Pain was her only constant

For days, she couldn't move without wanting to scream. When the aches started to ease, the fever began. She lost track of time, the edge between darkness and day blurring until she no longer knew or cared if the sun or the moon shone.

The hut where she lay was thatched and a mosquito net covered the space above her. There was nothing in the room but her bed and a small table beside it. In contrast, a window opening to the right framed a scene that looked more like a Gauguin painting than any place she'd ever been.

A woman came in several times a day and checked on her. Sometimes in the middle of the night—or maybe the middle of the day, she wasn't sure which—a man came, too. He was lean and gaunt with sunken eyes that frightened her. He never spoke. He did nothing but look at her.

She didn't know where she was.

She didn't know *who* she was.

Dear Reader,

Machu Picchu is a magical place. Set high in the mountains of Peru, near the city of Cuzco, these ancient ruins provide a glimpse into the world of the Incas. The city sprawls over five square miles and was built sometime in the 1400s, providing a home to over a thousand people. Cuzco was seized in 1534 by the conquering Spanish armies but Machu Picchu itself was not discovered until 1911 by Yale's Hiram Bingham.

I had the opportunity to visit Machu Picchu a few years ago. The buildings are incredible with intricate stonework and classic design, but even more impressive is the serenity the site seems to exude. The minute I began to climb the first set of terraced stairs (there are over three thousand steps at Machu Picchu!) I felt an eerie kind of calm. I was excited about being there but underneath that eagerness to explore, I experienced an emotion that has stayed with me ever since. I wished then (and even more so now) that I could have bottled that reaction.

A believer in reincarnation might attribute my response to the idea that I had lived there in another life. I don't know how to explain it but I do know that I experienced something unique during that trip. The vision of those mountains rising from the early-morning mist is one I cherish. While I took some liberties with geography (Rojo and Qunico exist only in my imagination), the magic of Machu Picchu is definitely real.

Lauren Stanley goes to Peru to uncover her past. The tragic death of her mother has haunted her for years and Lauren returns to gain the understanding that has eluded her since childhood. Once there, Lauren meets not truth, but danger. Her life is saved only through the intervention of Armando Torres. Armando's a man of irony—he's a dedicated physician but when called to duty, his healing skills take a turn in the opposite direction. Together they must solve the mystery of Lauren's past.

One day I'd like to return to the ruins of Machu Picchu. They deserve more time than I had when I visited. Until then, I'll continue to read about this glorious place and study the culture of the Indians who once had the privilege of living there. I hope I've piqued your interest in it as well.

Kay David

NOT WITHOUT
THE TRUTH
Kay David

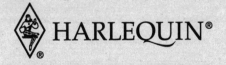

HARLEQUIN®

TORONTO • NEW YORK • LONDON
AMSTERDAM • PARIS • SYDNEY • HAMBURG
STOCKHOLM • ATHENS • TOKYO • MILAN • MADRID
PRAGUE • WARSAW • BUDAPEST • AUCKLAND

ISBN 0-373-78066-4

NOT WITHOUT THE TRUTH

Copyright © 2006 by Carla Luan.

This edition published by arrangement with Harlequin Books S.A.

® and TM are trademarks of the publisher. Trademarks indicated with
® are registered in the United States Patent and Trademark Office, the
Canadian Trade Marks Office and in other countries.

www.eHarlequin.com

Printed in U.S.A.

Books by Kay David

HARLEQUIN SUPERROMANCE

SIGNATURE SELECT SAGA

For Karen.
Thanks for all your help and expertise.
It's a joy to work with someone who understands
the need for special places where ideas can turn
into stories and naps are always encouraged.

PROLOGUE

Christmas Eve, 1989 U.S. Embassy
Lima, Peru

LAUREN WAS SUPPOSED to be asleep by
9:00 p.m., but Lauren seldom followed the
rules, especially dumb ones. It was Christmas eve, she'd complained to everyone
who would listen. Who went to bed at nine
on Christmas eve?

Ten-year-old girls do, her mother had
said, at least those who wanted to find
presents under the tree in the morning.

Margaret Stanley had tried to appear
stern and serious, but Lauren had heard the
softness behind her words. They both
knew that despite Lauren's behavior, her
Christmas was going to be a good one. Six

months ago, her mom had been appointed consul for Peru and she felt guilty for making Lauren and her dad leave their home in Dallas to come halfway around the world. Lauren had seen the stack of presents her mom had already wrapped.

Lauren played along, though. After her mom kissed her good-night and turned out the lamp, she closed her eyes and waited ten minutes, then she climbed from bed. Sneaking into the hallway, she peered up and down both ways before running to the iron railing that lined the upper gallery.

A crowd of glittering guests filled the huge reception area below, but as if he'd planned it, Daniel Cunningham, her mother's attaché, stood directly beneath where Lauren kneeled. His tuxedo was pressed, his shoes shone and he'd spiked his blond hair for the party. The style made him look even taller than he was and, gripping the black balusters, Lauren stared through the bars and sighed.

Okay, so he was old—at least twenty, maybe even twenty-five—*and* he worked for her mom, but he was *so* cool! Lauren had had a major crush on Daniel from the minute they'd arrived.

Normally her mom would have had a cow over Lauren's thing for Daniel but she'd overheard her parents talking, and her mom had admitted she was giving Lauren a pass because Daniel had managed to distract her. Lauren had bawled for days when she'd found out she was going to have to leave all her friends. Knowing there was no chance, she'd even begged to stay with her grandparents instead of moving. "We're a family," her mother had said. "And that means we stick together." Lauren had been really, really bummed. Until she'd spotted Daniel.

Daniel liked her, too. He treated her like she was a real person, not just some stupid kid who'd didn't have a choice about where she lived. He'd even taken the time to explain to her why it was important she and her dad be there. Her mother was an important person, Daniel had said solemnly, one of only three consuls who worked directly for the ambassador. The people of Peru saw the entire family as representatives of the United States. Daniel made her think she counted, something her mother never had the time to do.

Her mother came into view. She'd let Lauren pick out her dress for tonight, and it'd been no surprise which one she'd selected. The red beaded gown was Lauren's favorite and it fit her mom perfectly, the crystals shimmering and shining as she walked among her guests. She looked like a movie star. They didn't always get along, but her mom was really pretty neat and she was definitely awesome-looking.

In contrast, her father bobbed behind her like the little boat Lauren had played with in the bathtub when she was younger. He had on a tux like the other men, but the similarities stopped there. He wasn't elegant or even handsome and he sure didn't seem to be having a good time. Maybe his glasses made him look that way. More likely, it was his frown. Her father was a child psychiatrist and, back home, he'd taught other doctors at a fancy medical center how to treat crazy kids. He hadn't ever been a fun kind of dad, but since they'd come to South America, he'd stopped smiling completely. She'd even heard him yell at her mom once, something he'd never done in Dallas. Tonight he looked more uptight than usual.

He pretended he didn't see Lauren. He was angry at her, too, because she'd been such a toot about moving.

Her eyes searched the mob again. Daniel had moved closer to the dining room and another man, dressed in black, was standing beside him. She looked at Daniel but her gaze kept returning to the man with him. He was shorter than Daniel and Latin, his jacket filled out with muscles that Daniel could only dream of having. His black hair was long and slicked back and as she watched, he smoothed it, a gleam of gold on his wrist catching her attention. He looked kinda rough—like those drug lords on TV—and out of place next to the blond attaché.

Lauren edged closer to the wrought iron

so she could see better and when she did so, Daniel looked up, the white flash of her nightgown obviously drawing his notice. He smiled at her and lifted his glass as if in a salute. She wagged her fingers back at him, her heart doing a funny skipping thing inside her chest.

The man at Daniel's side raised his eyes, too. Lauren glanced in his direction, then something weird seemed to happen and she couldn't look away.

He was younger than she'd first thought, but his eyes didn't match the rest of him. Instead, they were like the old man's on the corner, the one who sold newspapers. He was about a hundred and he never seemed happy, not even when Lauren's dad gave him twice as big a tip as he should. Lauren's delight in being acknowledged by Daniel changed into confusion. The man scared her. Speaking to Daniel but keeping his eyes on hers, the stranger gestured. She had no idea who he was since she'd never seen him before, but she knew one thing: she didn't think she'd ever forget him.

Suddenly it seemed like a good time for Lauren to go.

She jumped up, her gown billowing around her legs as she ran, laughter and music from downstairs chasing her back to the private living quarters of the embassy. Her pulse racing as fast as her feet, she found herself in her mother's closet, the familiar scent of her perfume reassuring. Lauren sat down on the floor behind the louvered doors and prayed for the jittery feeling to leave.

She kept telling herself she wasn't afraid, until she fell into a fitful sleep, her dreams full of men with golden eyes. When she woke up to loud voices, it took her a moment to remember where she was. The conversation came to her in snatches.

"Dammit, Margaret, you don't understand…. Big mistake if you think…Lots of money to be made…."

Lauren started to call out but the argument held her back. Peeking through the slats in the door, she could see a pair of men's shoes and the hem of her mother's red gown. The man kinda sounded like Daniel but not really. Daniel never used bad words like *dammit* and his voice was higher than this man's.

"…not in the foreign service for money. I love my country…."

Lauren teased her mom sometimes and called her General Mother. No matter what, she stayed the same, strong, brave, no-nonsense. She was acting that way now. Taking a step toward the closet door, her mother spoke without hesitation.

"You aren't going to get away with this. I found out and others will, too."

"They won't if you aren't talking."

The man had come nearer, too, but Lauren still couldn't tell if it was Daniel or not. He sounded really scary and she thought about the stranger she'd seen beside Daniel. The man with the bracelet. Lauren heard him pull something from his pocket.

Her mother's gasp turned Lauren's

stomach inside out. She gripped a handful of carpet, her mouth going dry.

Her mother spoke slowly and calmly, just like she did when she was trying to explain something to Lauren. "Don't be stupid. That's not going to help things."

"I can see how you'd feel that way," the man said. "But I disagree."

A muffled pop followed.

Lauren scrambled backward so fast she almost hit the wall. Squeezing her eyes shut, she curled into a tiny ball and wedged herself as far as she could into the darkness where she tried not to think about what that noise meant. Part of her understood but a desperate sense of survival kept her silent. Over the ringing in her ears, she thought she heard the bedroom door open and close but she couldn't tell for sure, especially when she heard the sound again a few minutes later. Rocking back and forth, she moaned softly.

Five minutes passed. Maybe five hours.

Her mother always preached that procrastination only made things worse but something told Lauren "worse" was already on the other side of the closet door. She waited for as long as she dared, then she forced herself to move. She had to find out what had happened. Crawling on all fours like the baby she wished she still was, she reached the front of the closet and pushed the doors open.

Her mother lay on the floor, a red stain the color of her dress soaking the rug by her head.

A man bent over her, two fingers pressed to her throat. He wore black from head to toe, including a mask that completely covered his face.

Through the eye holes, the man's startled gaze met Lauren's. He jerked his hand away from her mother's neck, a gold glint at his wrist catching Lauren's attention.

For one long second, she was frozen. She couldn't move, she couldn't talk, she couldn't even breathe. The man went still, too.

Lauren didn't understand what happened next but she knew the moment would never leave her. She could hear his heartbeat, she realized with shock, and the quick intake of breath that *he* took filled *her* lungs. He sensed the connection as well and his gaze came alive.

They stared at each other another two seconds, then he pivoted and dashed to the nearest window. Lauren closed her eyes and began to scream.

CHAPTER ONE

Summer 2005
Near Machu Picchu

THE ROPE BRIDGE SWUNG LAZILY in the bright Peruvian sun. Every so often, a loose strand of hemp would free itself and float on the warm breeze before drifting away. Most of the strings fell to the river thirty feet below where the water rolled over the rocks in an easy rhythm. No hurry, the gentle rippling sound seemed to say, no rush.

On either side of the precarious walkway, scarlet macaws preened in the warmth, their iridescent feathers flashing against the thick green foliage like priceless jewels. The birds' exotic calls filled the air, along with the perfume from the nearby balsam trees.

Pausing on the edge of the gorge, Lauren Stanley studied the tranquil scene spread out before her. For as far as she could see, serenity and beauty lay. Breathing deeply, she tried to trap the essence of the moment and transfer its peace to a spot inside herself.

She failed.

All Lauren could feel was the fright that had her nailed to one spot. Big spiders and heights, tight spots and snakes. Lauren's list of fears was a long one and there were some things on it she couldn't even name. Despite their numbers, she'd managed to face most of them because she was too stubborn to give up on something just because it was difficult. The perfect example of that was right ahead of her. Seeing the ancient ruins of Machu Picchu would have been a straight-forward journey, but she'd had to come to the lesser ruins first, even though it had meant hacking a path through the jungle and crossing remote bridges like the one she was staring at now.

A second passed and then another one. Finally, she managed to break her paralysis. Opening her eyes, she lifted her hands and stared at them. They trembled violently, as did her body.

Behind her, Joaquin, the guide she'd hired, said something encouraging. At least, that's how she interpreted it. He spoke almost no Spanish and they'd had to make do between his Quechuan and sign language. She looked over her shoulder and the young man made a go-ahead motion with his hand. She faced forward once more and eased her right foot out.

The bridge was made of three ropes, two that acted as handrails and one Lauren would have to balance on as she walked across. They were lashed together with extra fibers at gaping intervals. The woven strand beneath her boot was probably two inches in diameter, maybe three at the most. She had forty feet to go and there was no other way to get to the other side.

She knew she shouldn't, but Lauren glanced down. The space beneath her seemed to widen and the green cliffs on either side shifted accordingly. A sickening dizziness swamped her.

I can't do this. She shut her eyes again. *I can't do this. What was I thinking? Why did I come here? Am I crazy or what?*

The questions were rhetorical because she knew the answer to each. She'd come back to Peru because she wasn't going to spend the rest of her life living in fear. She refused to. She'd spent enough time there and she was ready to move on. She had a great career ahead of her and nothing but opportunity. All she had to do was conquer the final frontier—her past. And she probably *was* nuts, but that had never stopped her.

Enough thinking, it was time to go. Lifting her left foot, Lauren carefully placed it in front of her right. She was near enough to the metal rings that held the ropes steady that the bridge stayed immobile under her shifting weight and her confidence took a step forward as well.

She continued, blanking her mind to anything but reaching the other side.

Measure by measure. Heartbeat by heartbeat. Breath by breath.

She was halfway across when the rope's tension seemed to change. Gripping the side ropes tightly, she told herself she was imagining things. Then the birds became quiet.

Turning her head slowly—it seemed to take a year—she glanced behind her. Joaquin was gone, the platform where the guide had been waiting now empty.

She puzzled over his disappearance. Maybe he'd slipped behind the foliage for a moment's privacy…. Maybe he'd sat down on the forest floor to wait for his turn to cross…. Maybe he'd gone back to his village and left her to her own devices…. She couldn't reverse her steps so she looked the way she'd been heading and tried to calm her concerns.

Then the rope bucked.

It steadied almost instantly and she sucked in a gasp of relief but before she could exhale, the cables went completely slack.

She screamed in terror as air replaced the support at her feet. The rope swung wildly and, burdened with her weight, headed for the rocks in front of her. If she held on, she'd slam into the side of the cliff.

The rough hemp burned through her palms, peeling the flesh from her fingers and setting them on fire with pain. The overhang zoomed closer. A tree branch, reaching out from the precipice as if to help, scraped her cheek instead.

A thousand different scenarios careered through her head but she knew she only had one choice. She held on until the last possible moment, but she finally opened her hands and let go.

She shrieked all the way down and hit the water with a splash. There was silence after that. When the last echo died, the birds resumed their calls.

"How you doing? Seen any ruins lately?"

Meredith Santera spoke in a casual way but Armando Torres wasn't fooled by her tone. Meredith wasn't a woman who telephoned just to chitchat. Her intensity never abated and she remained focused at all times. On occasion, she pretended otherwise, but in reality, she never let up.

"Why do you wake me in the middle of the night to ask how I feel?" A native of Argentina, Armando's accent became more obvious. "I think you have something other than my welfare on your mind."

A pause came over the line before she answered. "How come you say so little but understand so much?"

He made a sound of dismissal. "If you listened more and spoke less, you would hear what I hear. I have no special skills."

"I disagree, which is exactly why I've called you."

He waited in silence.

"I had an interesting conversation yesterday," she began.

Armando heard the sound of shuffling papers and he imagined Meredith sitting at her desk in Miami. She'd moved there after she'd left the CIA and started the Operatives. At the beginning, there had been four of them—Meredith, Armando and two others, Stratton O'Neil and Jonathan

Cruz—but in the past few years, some changes had come about.

Stratton had been the first to leave. Following a job that had gone tragically wrong, he'd moved to L.A. to escape his past and disengage from life. His plan had been foiled when he'd taken one last job then had fallen in love. Cruz had been next. He was teaching at Langley now and he, too, had a new wife. She happened to be Meredith's best friend. Cruz had married her after he'd rescued her and her son from the drug kingpin who was the child's father.

Armando had also wondered from time to time about leaving the team. He had more work at the clinic than he could handle and it was good work, productive work. But what he did with the Operatives was important, and he wasn't sure he could ever give it up.

Meredith's voice brought him back. "I got a call from a doctor in Dallas by the name of J. Freeman Stanley. He's a very well-known child psychiatrist. His expertise is in repressed memories. Does his name sound familiar?"

Armando held his breath, his past rising up from the grave where he kept it buried. "Not really," he lied.

"You'll remember when you hear the rest. You must be getting old."

I am, he thought, *and growing even more so as you speak.* He'd never told Meredith much about his early years. Her father had helped her form the company and he'd been the one she'd trusted to choose the men. He'd known everyone's secrets but he was gone now. All Meredith knew was that Armando had been involved with the Peruvian job. She had no idea he'd seen the girl. No one knew that, except for him and her.

"Dr. Stanley has a daughter named Lauren," she said. "Her mother was Margaret Stanley." Meredith paused. "Don't tell me you don't remember her. She was—"

"One of the consuls in Lima." He dropped his pretense. "Christmas eve, 1989. I was sent there that night, but she was already dead before I could get to her. They said she interrupted a burglar and he killed her. I remember."

"Finally! I was getting worried about you for a minute."

He interrupted her, an act of discourtesy he'd normally never indulge in. "What's wrong?"

If she noticed his shortness, she ignored it. "Lauren Stanley is twenty-six now. She's a writer for a travel magazine called *Luxury* and she's been on assignment in Peru doing an article about the ruins."

"*Luxury*, eh?" Armando forced the tightness in his chest to loosen. "That sounds like a nice job. To visit rich people's resorts and write about them."

"It *sounds* good, yes, but something must have happened. About two weeks ago, she stopped checking in and her father is getting frantic."

"How did he connect with you?"

"He didn't. My father was still in Washington when Stanley's wife died and Dad debriefed the doctor after he and his daughter left Peru. According to Stanley, Dad told him if there was ever anything he could do for him to call. So he did. The office forwarded the message to me. Stanley had no idea that my father was dead."

Her voice seemed to thicken but Armando knew he was imagining the sound. Meredith's emotions were so tightly controlled he didn't think she even knew *how* to feel them anymore.

"And what does this have to do with me?"

"She's missing. You're there. I thought you could at least ask around—"

"She is a grown woman," Armando said sharply. "She probably found a lover and ran off with him."

"I hope so, but the situation's a little more complicated than it appears. Freeman Stanley said the mother's death left Lauren Stanley unstable and prone to depression. Considering her past, I think he has a right to be concerned. I would be if she were my daughter. So would you."

Outside his open bedroom window, somewhere in the undergrowth beyond, Armando heard the foliage rustle and the low grunt of an animal. He didn't try to guess what it was. The rugged mountainous terrain provided a home for many living things, as well as for some things that weren't. The Quechuan were a superstitious lot, but not without good reason.

Meredith's voice held her first hint of impatience. "Have you seen anything—"

"I'm not that close to Machu."

"No, but you're not that far and a lot of people visit those smaller ruins close to where you live, too. She could have done that."

"It's possible," he said reluctantly, "but I've heard nothing."

"When was the last time you went into the village?"

The clinic was located near a dot on the map called Rojo. It was located between Cuzco and the ruins of Machu Picchu. "I haven't been to Rojo in a month," he said. "Maybe two. I forget."

Meredith made a tsk-tsking sound. "You're turning into *el ermitaño,* Armandito…."

"A hermit is better than what they call me now."

"The locals still think you can make yourself invisible?"

"They must," he said with a shrug. "Nothing but *el médico del fantasma* could do so, I presume."

"You need to get out more," she remarked. "Go to Rojo for me. Be my ears and eyes. I want to call this man and help him out."

"And if we cannot do that?"

"Then I'll tell him that, too," she said. "But you have to ask around first. I don't want to lie to him either way."

Armando sighed. He didn't want to get involved, but guilt was a powerful motivator—and a heavy weight. Of all the cases in his past, why had this one come back? He'd lost more sleep over the little girl with the haunting eyes than he had over any of his other assignments.

"How would I know her?" he asked reluctantly.

"I'll fax you a photo. She won't be hard to miss. Believe me, if she's anywhere around there, you'll know. She's gorgeous. Blond, blue eyes, thin. She looks like a supermodel." Meredith hesitated, then corrected herself. "No, wait. Actually, that's not quite true. She looks like her mother. Exactly like her. Do you remember her?"

"Yes."

Oblivious to what his one-syllable answer signified, Meredith continued. "Maybe you'll fall in love with her," she teased. "And move back to the States like Cruz and Stratton. You could have three children and buy a big ranch in Texas. You'd make lots of money, you know."

"I need no more money," he said, staring out into the night. "And I don't want a wife and three children. Or a ranch in Texas."

Finally sensing his mood, she spoke with a serious tone. "Then what *do* you want, Armando? Cruz has found his place in the world and Stratton has gotten himself straightened out. They seem happy. When are you going to give up being the broody Latin and do the same?"

"I'm thrilled for them," he said. "But I'm not sure that condition will ever find me."

"It doesn't just fall into your lap," she said sharply. "You have to search for it."

"You're correct as usual," he said. "But I carry too many images of death. They visit me without invitation and linger in the corners. I don't need to look for anything more, much less happiness. "

"We've done a lot of good, Armando."

"I know that. I'm still a believer, don't worry."

"Then concentrate on that. Otherwise, you'll drive yourself insane."

"Your advice is wise, Meredith, but it comes too late." His voice went quiet and low with regret. "I've done things I shouldn't have and left too many other things undone."

They hung up without saying goodbye. A moment later, the fax on his desk rang shrilly. Armando walked to the machine and watched the picture of Lauren Stanley emerge, line by line. When the photo was complete, he continued to stare. Meredith had been correct. The little girl he'd seen had turned into a stunning woman. If she was anywhere near Rojo or even Aquas Caliente, the larger village upriver, he would have heard by now.

Picking up the fax, he crumpled it out of habit then put a match to the wad of paper. White ash fell like snow into the metal wastebasket at his feet.

He went back to bed but sleep didn't join him.

SHE DIDN'T KNOW where she was.

Pain was her only constant. For days, she hadn't been able to move without wanting to scream. When the aches had started to ease, the fever had begun. She'd lost track of time, the edge between darkness and day blurring until she no longer knew—or cared—if the sun or the moon shone.

The hut where she lay was thatched and a mosquito net covered the space above her. There was nothing in the room but her bed and a small table beside it. In contrast, a window opening to the right framed a scene that looked more like a Gauguin painting than any actual place she'd ever been.

A woman came in several times a day and checked on her. Sometimes in the middle of the night—or maybe the middle of the day, she wasn't sure which—a man came, too. He was lean and gaunt with sunken eyes that frightened her. He never spoke. He did nothing but look at her.

She didn't know where she was.

She didn't know *who* she was.

THE DAY AFTER MEREDITH CALLED, Armando went into Rojo, but no one in the village had seen a *gringa*. He returned home and put the woman out of his mind. When Meredith called a week later, he told her he knew nothing.

"Dammit, I hate having to call Freeman Stanley and tell him that. Are you sure no one's seen her?"

He let his silence answer the question.

"What should I do?" she asked in a worried voice.

He shook his head at her ploy. "Don't try

to pull one of your tricks on me, Meredith. You asked me to see if Lauren Stanley had been here and that is what I did. If this was a real assignment, I would stop and do anything you asked, you know that, but otherwise my days here are very full already. I have the clinic and the villages and the children. I did not join the Operatives to find missing daughters for worried daddies."

"Stanley has called me too many times to count. He offered us a lot of money."

"And I told you last time we spoke that I have no need of that."

"Maybe *you* don't," she said, "but what about your clinic? When I saw you at Cruz's wedding, you said the place continuously required new equipment and stronger drugs and more staff and better beds—"

He interrupted her as she had him. "The funds this man could give us wouldn't make a dent in what we lack. And the time it would take to do the job, to find this woman, I do not have it, Meredith."

"Your time I can't replace," she said.

"But you're wrong about the money." She named a figure that shocked him. "You could buy a lot of aspirin with that, Armando. A donation that size could keep the clinic running for years. You could even hire another doctor." She paused then added in a mocking voice, "A *real* doctor."

Armando was a psychiatrist and Meredith liked to tease him about it. He ignored her taunt this time, however, and thought of the infant he'd seen yesterday. One listen through his stethoscope and he'd known that the child had a serious heart defect, probably congenital. Other symptoms had confirmed his suspicions—the pale skin, the wheezing breath, the lethargy. Any medium-size hospital in the States could have corrected the problem, but here the baby had no chance.

"I'll call you in two days." He made the promise abruptly then hung up.

Later that morning, his housekeeper, who also served as a nurse at the clinic, came to his study. Zue was Quechuan and eighty. She worked hard but her grandson,

Beli, who also helped around the compound, did just the opposite. Knowing Armando would pay him regardless, he put out as little effort as possible.

"There are people here," she sniffed. "From Qunico. I told them the clinic was closed but they won't go away. They're farmers."

Armando had learned a long time ago not to point out what he thought were the discrepancies in Zue's complicated class hierarchy. "Send them in," he said.

Under Zue's watchful eyes, the two men shuffled inside. Wrapped in woven blankets, they were exhausted and filthy. Qunico was fifty miles east of Rojo and even if they had had a vehicle, there was nothing but a rough path between the two. They'd either walked or ridden mules. Armando studied them but they both seemed healthy.

The taller of two spoke haltingly. "*Señor Doctor,* we have a woman in our village. She is hurt and very sick. She needs your help. You are the only one who can save her."

Armando stilled. Something inside told him he knew the answer to his question, but he asked it anyway. "The woman is a *gringa*, no? With blond hair and *ojos azules?*"

The men exchanged a startled look and Armando realized he'd just added to the rumors that swirled about him. They came to him for help, but most of the villagers were frightened of him—they thought he could read their minds, disappear at will and heal with a touch. He didn't like the mystery they'd built up around him, but sometimes it proved useful, he had to admit.

"What's wrong with her?" Armando asked.

Their explanation came out in a jumble of Spanish and Quechuan but even if one language had prevailed, it wouldn't have mattered. They were too overwhelmed to get the tale told in any kind of order. Armando held his hand up after a few moments and halted the flow.

"*Por favor, amigos,* one thing at a time. Start at the beginning."

The taller man, clearly the leader, paused

and tried to organize his thoughts. Finally he shook his head in a gesture of defeat. "We don't know the beginning, señor."

Armando frowned. "What do you mean?"

"We don't know where she came from or how she escaped, but Xuachoto had her in his arms for a very long time. We think maybe he wanted to claim her for a new bride, but Mariaita wouldn't let him. He had to give her up."

The locals followed a convoluted mixture of Catholicism and Inca myths that had evolved through the centuries, their leader, Manco, serving as both priest and mayor. Armando hadn't bothered to study the intricacies of the system but some of his ignorance was not his own fault. When the clinic had opened and the locals had seen what Armando's medicines could do, they'd begun to bypass the old man's rites and gone directly to Armando's clinic for healing. In return, Manco deliberately made things more difficult because he resented what he perceived to be Armando's healing powers and was jealous of his abilities.

Armando knew enough to recognize the name of their water god, Xuachoto, though, and his jealous wife, Mariaita. A chill came over him despite the heat and he dreaded hearing the answer to his next question.

"Are you telling me the *gringa* was in the river when you found her?"

They nodded in unison, then the shorter man spoke reverently. "Xuachoto had her. Manco fought hard, but he couldn't bring her back from the other side. We know *you* can do better."

"She's dead?" Armando asked in alarm.

"No, señor, she is not dead." He sent an uneasy look to his companion then faced Armando again. "But she is not alive, either."

CHAPTER TWO

WHEN SHE FIRST HEARD the voices, she thought she was dreaming, then she became more aware of her surroundings and realized her mistake.

"I can take care of her," a man said. "Your assistance is not needed here. They should never have bothered you with this."

She struggled to open her eyes, her lids weighed down by sleep and pain. The man who spoke was the one she'd seen come into her tent before. His voice reverberated with a frightening kind of fervor.

"I am confident that you are able to handle the situation, Manco." The second man answered in the same language of the first—Spanish—but his voice was much kinder, its tones softened by a sophisticated accent and polished manner. "I mean no disrespect. I merely want to help."

She fought against her stupor and forced her eyes to stay open so she could study the visitor. His eyes were two black stones, polished and bright, his skin a burnished brown, his hair straight and black. He had the right coloring but she didn't think he was local. For one thing, he wore American jeans and a T-shirt. Her guess was based on his attitude rather than what he had on, however. He had an air of authority about him, a self-confidence that told her he wasn't about to give in to the man who stood before him. Her eyes shut again.

"I brought her back from the dead." The tall man's voice penetrated her fog but just barely. "If not for me, she would be in the ground at this very moment. Her family would be crying and lighting candles."

"That may be true," the stranger replied politely. "But you can't talk to her and I can."

"I speak the language of healing. English isn't necessary."

A paused filled the hut. As it grew, she

beat her lethargy and turned to look at them again. The two men stared at each other, their faces filled with tension, and as she watched, the American, which she guessed him to be, stepped even closer to the older man, their chests now almost touching. His voice was so low she could hardly make out what he said. The steady conviction behind it, however, was unmistakable.

"You're a very busy man, Manco. You have the farm to run, the animals to oversee, your people to guide. I'm sure you could handle this problem, but you don't need another person to look after." He paused, his silky voice at once respectful but threatening. "The burden of the woman's care would require too much of your valuable attention. Your village could suffer. Your men were thinking of you when they came and asked for my assistance."

He was offering a way to save face, which was nice because the outcome of this argument was not in question. The American was going to get what he wanted, in any event. For some reason, she suspected that was not unusual.

She didn't know what Manco saw as he studied the man's face but he must have read something in his expression that gave him pause. After a moment so long Lauren wasn't sure it would end, he stepped back and held out his hand. "You are right, Doctor, as usual. Your wisdom far out-weighs my own. I had not thought of the problem in those terms."

The man in the T-shirt shook his head. "No one's wisdom is greater than yours, Manco. The problem is your heart. It is too big. You try to help everyone."

"You flatter me, but I will accept your praise." The man smiled as he spoke but it wasn't genuine. He wasn't happy, yet there was nothing more that he could do. He waved his hand in dismissal and turned to leave. "I'll send someone to help carry her out."

Before Manco had even left the hut, the doctor, if that's what he was, was at the edge of her bed and lifting the mosquito netting. He appeared pleased by her open eyes.

"You're awake. That is good. Very good. You didn't seem to know I was here when I first arrived and examined you."

He stuck out his hand and confirmed his title. "I'm Armando Torres. I'm going to take you to my clinic so I can see to your injuries. It's not far from here. Do you think you can make it?"

She attempted to speak but all that came out was a croak.

"Save your energy." He brushed a curl of her hair off her forehead in a soothing gesture, misinterpreting her effort. "We don't need to be polite. The niceties can wait."

She *had* to try again. "Do you…"

He put his fingers over hers, his kind manner and authoritative air instantly winning her trust. "Do I what?" he asked, his eyes puzzled.

Her gaze fastened on his as if she could pull the answer from him. "Do you know who I am?"

ARMANDO STARED DOWN at Lauren Stanley in shock. When the men who'd retrieved him had said she wasn't alive, he hadn't understood. Defensive and angry, Manco had explained the situation with more arrogance than usual and left out the details as well. The Quechuan believed in more than a single state of being, he'd said haughtily, and Lauren's ailment reflected one that was highly mystical. Armando had accepted the lecture, but he'd had no idea Manco had been referring to amnesia.

"You don't know your name?" he asked in surprise.

She shook her head then winced at the movement. She was so pale beneath her tan, Armando thought he could see through her skin.

"I can remember a few things," she said haltingly. "But I don't know why I'm here or what I do."

She waited for him to fill her in but Armando didn't answer right away. Beneath the pallor and grime, she certainly looked like the photo Meredith had sent him, but Armando didn't like to make assumptions and he wasn't about to start now. "Did you have things with you?" he asked instead.

"I don't know." A look of frustration crossed her delicate features. "I tried to ask, but my sign language skills aren't too good."

Armando walked to the doorway. Tiachita, Manco's housekeeper, lounged on the porch, her need for activity apparently less developed than Zue's. She looked up as he spoke.

"Did the blonde have anything with her? A bag? Papers? Anything?"

Tiachita stood with a languid grace and walked to the kitchen of the hut, which was housed in a separate building off to one side. She returned a second later and handed him a small ripped windbreaker.

"This is it?"

She gave him the exact reply he'd expected. A slow nod of her head. He cursed beneath his breath and retraced his steps, flipping open the coat as he walked. If Lauren Stanley had fallen in the river with an entire suite of Vuitton luggage, the answer would have been the same. Unattended items didn't last long in this part of the world. He was surprised even to have this.

He paused on the front porch and looked at the inside tag. Someone had written Lauren Stanley, Dallas, Texas, in small block letters at the top in indelible ink. Luxury had been printed underneath her name.

"There's nothing left," he declared when he came back to her side, "except this."

She raised her head. "A ratty jacket? That's it?"

He nodded as she fought to focus, her small source of energy obviously depleted.

"There's a name on the tag," he said.

In the dim light, her blue eyes seemed to glow. "What is it?"

"Lauren Stanley," he said. "'Dallas, Texas' is written just below it."

She repeated what he'd said then her eyes filled. "I've never heard that name before," she whispered. "If that's who I am, it's news to me."

LAUREN STANLEY DROPPED BACK into a fitful sleep and Armando began to organize the trip back to the clinic. It would have taken less than an hour in an ambulance, but patient transportation here had as much in common with its international counterparts as he did with Manco.

Lining the wooden floor of a cart with pillows and blankets, the men made a bed for Lauren, then attached the rig to the back of Armando's battered motorcycle. When they finished, he stared at it and shook his head. She was going to feel every bump and rut in the path between Qunico and the clinic but he couldn't give her anything to knock her out. Until he had a better handle on her injuries, he couldn't risk the complications that might arise.

He went back inside and found her sitting on the edge of the bed, holding her head in her hands. Tiachita stood beside her. "Very dizzy," the housekeeper said. "Very bad. No can walk."

Tiachita seemed to support her boss's bid to keep Lauren. Ignoring her try,

Armando took a bottle of water from his backpack and handed it to Lauren. "You're probably dehydrated," he said. "It comes up on you fast out here."

She accepted the water without comment, her dazed state and slowed movements disturbing to him. Had she hit her head while she'd been in the water? He hadn't been able to see any signs of contusions but reactions to injuries like that could be delayed. A whole host of other possibilities raced through his mind, some of them with outcomes that could be very serious.

He capped the water bottle and dropped it into his pack. "You ready?"

Instead of answering, she tried to stand, but she swayed instead, her legs going out from beneath her. Grabbing her arms, Armando caught her just before she went down completely.

"Oh, God," she murmured. "I think the woman is right. No can walk."

Armando chuckled. "You don't have to

walk. I'm going to carry you. Just put your arms around my neck."

She did as he instructed and he lifted her easily. Too easily. She'd probably carried ten pounds more before her accident. She'd lost none of her beauty, though. The luminous skin, the clear blue eyes, the heart-shaped face, they were all there now, the promise he'd seen in her features as a child now fulfilled.

When he laid her in the cart she groaned and curled on her side. Rearranging the pillows to better cushion her, Armando said a quick prayer then straddled the cycle and aimed it down the path.

THEIR RETURN WASN'T as bad as Armando had thought it would be. Maybe the Quechuan gods *were* impressed with Lauren Stanley's altered state. Whatever it was, Armando didn't care. He was grateful they got back to the clinic before nightfall. He'd been stranded before in the night in the surrounding jungle and it hadn't been fun. The experience wouldn't have been any better with an injured woman to care for.

The muffled hum of his motorcycle shattered the quiet as he pulled into the clinic's compound. Zue hurried out to meet him, her tongue clicking before he could say anything. With a flick of her wrist, she had three men out to help. They gently lifted the blonde and carried her inside while Zue berated them the entire distance, cautioning them not to bump the patient while at the same time hurrying them toward the clinic's four-bed hospital. Armando shook the dust from his clothing and went to clean himself up. Zue would bathe Lauren, then he'd examine her. They never had too many patients at one time but there was generally a steady stream. He and his nurse had their routine down.

He was stepping out of the shower when his cell phone rang. Seeing the caller ID number, he picked up the phone and, without thinking, fell into the coded speech he and Meredith used when discussing a job.

He greeted her, then said, "I have the package you were looking for—it was found late yesterday afternoon. Apparently it'd been around for a while but I hadn't heard."

She followed his lead, her voice relieved. "Armando, that's great! It wasn't…damaged, was it?"

"There's some dents and scratches on the outside but I believe everything is okay on the inside. I haven't had a chance to open it yet and see."

"Where was it all this time?"

"It's a long story," he said. "I'll call you later when the rates go down and explain." This meant he'd e-mail her, but as he expected, Meredith didn't have the patience for that.

"Tell me now," she insisted. "The manufacturer wants to know."

"It got wet," he said with a sigh, "and had to be fished out of a nearby river. I'm not sure how it ended up there, but that's basically what happened."

"But it's okay?" she asked again.

He hesitated and tried to think of a way

to avoid the topic of Lauren's amnesia. He needed to examine her before he could address that subject adequately, but his reluctance went beyond that. Something about the situation had begun to bother him during the trip home, but he couldn't yet define what it was.

"Basically, it is okay. Yes." He paused and Meredith sensed that he was holding something back.

"But?"

He licked his lips and stared out the window beside the desk where he stood. Night came swiftly in Peru and it was totally black outside now. He'd never seen a place with such an absence of light and he'd been in plenty of dark places in his life.

"I think it might be best if you could wait a bit before calling the manufacturer."

"Why is that?" Her voice took on a puzzled but cautious note. "He's quite anxious to hear any news we can give him."

"I can see why," Armando replied, "but something doesn't feel right. You know what I mean?"

"I probably do," she said with a weary sigh. "I'll hold off if you think that's best."

"I do," he said. "But I can't give you a reason why right now. Maybe later I'll understand better." His eyes searched the void through the screen. "And then again," he added, "maybe I won't."

SHE REMEMBERED LITTLE about the journey yet, when she woke up the following morning, she felt as if she'd moved across the world instead of across the valley.

She sat up in the bed and took in her surroundings. The clinic was spotless, the walls a white so stark they hurt her eyes, the floors so clean, she was sure they would squeak if walked on. There were three other beds in the room along with her own but they were empty.

The simple task of looking around took most of her energy and she fell back against the pillows. Her eyes didn't open again until that evening when a tiny native woman came in with a dinner tray, the china and cutlery arranged with military precision. She insisted on feeding Lauren, then returned the next morning to do the same with breakfast. The doctor came twice, but each time she registered little more than the fact that he was examining her, his hands gliding over her bruised body with care, his voice comforting as he murmured to her.

On her third morning, she woke up with a much clearer mind. Recalling the name the doctor had told her was hers, she probed her memory for more details.

She had little success.

All she could force out was a murky mix of faces and facts that made no sense, each changing rapidly, and feeling more like bad dreams than memories.

That night, after she'd bathed Lauren and cleaned up the ward with the endless energy she seemed to have, the nurse began to braid Lauren's hair. She was almost finished when the doctor came in.

Clearly upset by the intrusion, she finished her task and stomped from the room.

The doctor watched her leave before

turning to Lauren with a bemused expression on his face. "I'm sorry to interrupt your salon time with Zue."

Lauren found herself smiling in return. "She's more upset than I am, believe me. My hair is the last thing on my mind right now, Dr. Torres."

"Please call me Armando." He pulled up a chair and sat down. "We do not stand on formality here."

She wasn't sure but yesterday, or maybe it'd been the day before, she'd realized he had a hint of an accent. She'd asked about it, and he'd explained he'd grown up in Argentina.

He looked at her intently. "So how are you feeling?"

Lauren had begun to realize Armando Torres had a habit of focusing on her so intently that she found it difficult to look away from him when he was anywhere near. Which wasn't a bad thing. Armando was a man anyone could have stared at for a long time and Lauren was surprised to find herself attracted to him. She'd explained the reaction by connecting it to her weakened state, but she knew better. There was something about him that felt familiar…yet strange, and the combination was a powerful one.

"I actually feel better," she said. Some of her aches weren't as sharp and some of her bruises had started to fade. "I was doubtful there for a while but it looks like I might survive."

"There was never any danger of that. The rough-est part is behind you."

"That was right after they pulled me from the water?" He'd told her the circumstances of her discovery.

"Yes. You were very lucky, you know. That's not a river you would have chosen to go into, if you'd known how bad it is."

"What do you mean? What's wrong with it?"

"Besides the usual piranha-crocodile-snake thing?"

She arched one eyebrow. "Uh-oh."

"A lot of bacteria thrive there that live nowhere else. I won't go into the details, but they can enter your body in various ways and then they set up housekeeping. Getting rid of them can be tricky. You have to catch them early or they can do a lot of damage to your internal organs, especially to your heart."

"I didn't know that," she said. "At least I don't think I did." Failing to keep the defeat from her voice, she spoke again. "I can't believe this! Amnesia is something you see in movies or read about in books—it's not supposed to happen to real people."

"The condition has been glamorized," he agreed, "but it obviously does affect 'real' people. It's affected you."

His reassurance made her feel much better but she immediately wondered why. She'd known the man for only a few days. How could he have such sway over her so quickly? "Will my memory ever come back?"

"I think that it will," he said. "But amnesia is one of those problems we still don't understand. If the source is organic—that is, you hit your head when you fell into the water and a physical part of your brain has been affected—your recovery time will be related to the damage that was done when you had the accident. If it's psychogenic, that's a different thing."

"'Psychogenic'? Meaning I'm making it happen to myself?"

"No. Psychogenic meaning the problem is psychologically based." He paused and appeared to think of how to phrase his explanation. "Psychogenic amnesia occurs after some sort of stress takes place. People who suffer this form of amnesia sometimes have a history of depression." His stare captured hers once again, the tension in the room notching up. "Psychogenic amnesia can be linked to suicide, as well."

IF HE HADN'T BEEN TRAINED to notice such things, Armando would have missed the reaction that crossed her expression, but his medical degree gave him an advantage.

As did his past.

Knowing what he did, he would have been surprised if she hadn't had some psy-

chological problems. Her issues had roots
that had been growing for years.

"Are you saying you think I was trying
to kill myself by jumping in the river?"
She didn't wait for him to answer. "If you
are, I have to disagree. I would have picked
a simpler way."

"That's not at all what I'm suggesting. I'm
merely trying to explain that amnesia is a
complex disease. You may not suffer from it
for very long, though. Sometimes all it takes
is a single detail and everything returns."

"But it's still frustrating."

"I imagine that it is, however, I may be
able to help you there. Your government
has been contacted by a man who claims
to be your father. He wanted help in
finding you, and the person who handled
the call knew of my clinic. She decided to
cut through the red tape and phone me first
to see if I'd heard anything."

Lauren's face filled with shock and she
struggled to sit up. "Are you kidding me?"

He shook his head. "Absolutely not."

"Oh, my God!" Her eyes huge, she

leaned forward as if she could get the information faster by being that much closer. "Who is my father? What was I doing here? Where is—"

Armando held up his hand. "I'll answer your questions the best I can, but I may not know everything—"

"I don't care! Just tell me!"

"Your name *is* Lauren Stanley and you *are* from Dallas. You're a writer, for a magazine called *Luxury,* and you were here on assignment to do an article about Machu Picchu and some of the other ruins. Your father is a doctor and he started to worry when you didn't call in as expected. Apparently you and he have some kind of system where you check in with him on a regular basis. He was afraid something had happened."

Her expression became remote. "What's his name?"

"J. Freeman Stanley."

"Does he know I'm all right?"

"He's been told. My friend said he was very relieved and he wants to talk to you as soon as possible. When we finish here, you can call him if you like."

He fell silent. She'd asked all the right questions, yet there was something missing. After a second, he realized what is was; none of the information he'd given her was resonating. Her expression held no reaction whatsoever. Normally he wouldn't have been surprised by that, but because of her eagerness, he expected disappointment from her, if nothing else.

"Does any of this sound familiar?" he asked, just to be sure.

She shook her head slowly. "You could be talking about a stranger for all I know."

Armando stood. "Don't worry about it for now," he ordered. "Once you speak with your father that could change."

Lauren opened her mouth to reply, but her expression went blank. Her eyes glazed over and became unfocused, then a second later, she jerked so hard the bed moved. Fearing a seizure or even something worse, Armando grabbed her shoulders and spoke her name loudly.

The episode was over almost before it began. She blinked then looked straight into his eyes and gasped.

"I was in a jungle and there were birds," she said. "Th-then I was flying."

He loosened his hold on her arms but he didn't release her. "You're *not* flying, Lauren," he said forcefully. "You're in bed. I have you. You're safe."

"It felt like I was looking at you behind a veil. I thought I was dreaming but it was more real."

"Describe what you saw."

"Thick foliage," she said haltingly. "The sound of birds, a rope sliding through my hands." She stopped abruptly and went silent, the intensity of the sensation obviously still frightening to her. "I was up high but I felt a rope," she said. "There was a rope in my hands!"

He took her hands and turned them over, shaking his head as he stared at the scabs that covered her palms. "I *thought* these were rope burns but then I convinced myself they were scratches from a tree limb you'd

tried to grab. I should have known better."
He raised his eyes to hers. "Someone must
have tried to help you after you fell into the
water. Was there anyone with you?"

She screwed up her face as if she could
force the memory out of her brain, but in
the end, all she could do was shake her
head. "I don't know! I guess anything's
possible, but I don't know."

He released her hands and patted her
arm, his reassurance swift and soothing. "It
will come to you," he said in a comforting
voice. "It will come."

"Is that a promise?"

"This is Peru," he answered cryptically.
"Promises are all that we have."

CHAPTER THREE

ARMANDO TORRES GAVE HER his cell phone then stepped outside as she dialed the number written on the small slip of paper he'd handed her. The first ring had barely finished when the phone was answered at the other end.

"Children's Clinic. How may I direct your call?"

"I need to speak with Dr. Stanley," Lauren said. "This is his daughter calling."

She felt strange describing herself as someone's daughter but as Lauren waited to talk to the man who claimed to be her father, she knew that Armando had told her the truth. She trusted him but she wasn't quite sure why.

"Lauren?"

She gripped the phone tighter as her name was spoken. "Y-yes," she managed to say. "This is Lauren."

"Oh, sweetheart! You don't know how worried I've been. Thank God you're all right! How do you feel? When are you coming home? They told me you lost all your things! Do you want me to come down and get you?"

The man at the other end stopped to take a breath and when he did so, he seemed to realize how rattled he sounded. He laughed apologetically. "I'm sorry—I know I'm running off at the mouth, but I'm just so relieved to know you're okay. Tell me how you feel."

"I'm still a little sore," she said, "but Dr. Torres has reassured me nothing's broken."

His voice was strained. "Is he taking good care of you?"

"Absolutely," she said. "Except that I have this… memory problem—"

Her father broke in, his tone switching to a more professional level. "I understand but I don't want you to worry about that,

Lauren, okay? It's a temporary setback and you're going to be fine. Once you're back home, we'll get you in to see Dr. Gladney right away. The two of you can work everything out, just like you did before. You'll be fine in no time."

To Lauren's ears, his manner seemed forced, but maybe he was simply overwhelmed with worry. "Dr. Gladney?"

"She's your therapist, honey. You don't remember her?"

"I don't remember me," Lauren replied, half joking, "how could I remember her?"

He took her question seriously and Lauren got the impression that he probably took most things that way. "Dr. Gladney is a specialist in psychotherapy as it relates to traumatic reassessments and integration, Lauren. She's worked with you for years, ever since—"

He broke off and Lauren asked, "Ever since what?"

For a moment, a static silence whispered down the line, then he spoke again. "Ever since your mother died. You don't remember that, either?"

A vague reaction tugged at the back of her mind—something forbidden and scary and chaotic. She tried hard to pull more out of the fleeting sensation but failed. "I'm sorry. I can't seem to…"

"It's okay." She could tell he was trying to hide his shock. "There'll be plenty of time to talk about that later."

Lauren pressed him. "Tell me now," she insisted. "Dr. Torres said all I might need is a single memory and everything else might come back. I want to know."

"It's complicated—"

"Then simplify it."

"All right," he said reluctantly. "The truth is your mother took her own life when you were ten. It was a very sad time for all of us and it was especially traumatic for you. You found the body."

"I—I can't believe I wouldn't remember something like that," she said in sudden shock. "It must have been horrible…"

He hurried to reassure her. "Your

reaction is extremely typical, Lauren. I'd be surprised if you *did* remember it. Don't worry about it, all right? We'll handle everything when you get back. Dr. Gladney and I will help you, I promise. You'll be fine as soon as we get you home."

He sounded as if he thought she were about to crash and burn. Losing your mother was a terrible thing but it'd clearly happened years before. He was acting as if he were afraid she might fall apart completely. What kind of fragile flower had she been?

"When do you think you can make it back to Cuzco?" Her father's question cut into her thoughts. "That's the largest town nearby. I've already checked the flights for you and there are some going out at the end of the week. I've wired some funds to you, as well. The doctor will collect them and get them to you. I know you lost your things. There should be more than enough cash for you to buy some clothes and anything else you might need until you come back but if you need more, let me know. I've contacted the embassy and your replacement passport is in the works. I'm not sure which flight would be the best but the earliest one is next—"

Lauren interrupted his flow of orders. "I'm not ready to come back. I have things to do here."

His voice revealed his surprise. "Lauren, don't be silly! You have to come home now. Forget about the article. The magazine doesn't expect you to finish that! I've already spoken to Neal—"

"Who's Neal?"

"Your boss," he answered. "He said the topic was all your idea anyway and he's not even sure when it would make the magazine. Your health is more important than writing—"

Lauren gripped the edge of the bed, the realization coming to her that she'd apparently allowed her father to tell her how to run her life. "I appreciate your help," she interrupted him one more time, "but I'm not coming back until I'm ready. I'll let you know when that is."

In the quiet that followed, she could

sense his disbelief. His voice changed subtly. "I really think you need to return, Lauren. You can't possibly get the care you need down there." He paused. "I'm a doctor myself, sweetheart, and I know what's best, especially for you. I'm sure Dr. Torres is…all right, but I know your case. After all, I'm your father. He's a stranger."

She looked out the screen door where Armando stood. Her father might be correct in what he said, but just the opposite felt true. She sensed no connection whatsoever with him but strangely enough, Armando Torres had seemed like someone she knew—and knew intimately—from the minute she had seen him. The idea was disturbing.

"I appreciate your concern," she repeated. "But I have things to do here. When they're done, I'll leave."

They hung up and Armando came in shortly after that for his phone. While Lauren got ready for bed, the dynamics of the conversation that had taken place between herself and the man who'd said he was her father replayed in her mind. She was a grown woman and had her wits about her—why did he feel the need to tell her what to do? Even more importantly, why did she feel the need to stay where she was? When he'd told her to come home, she'd declined instinctively. Why? She worried over the situation for a while longer, then sleep overcame her.

She woke abruptly at 2:30 a.m., her scream still echoing in the empty ward. Her hands gripped the edge of the bed so hard, the scrapes on her palms had opened and begun to bleed again.

A blond man had been leading her across a rope bridge. She was almost to the other side when he magically appeared on the bank ahead of her, but before she could reach him, the rope went slack. For two seconds, Lauren was suspended in space and then she was falling.

She blinked and the images faded but, without any warning, she recalled the moments before she'd gone into the water. She'd been going over the river on a rope bridge. And she'd fallen.

She sat up in excitement and swung her legs over the edge of the bed. The sheets and her hands were a mess but she barely noticed she was so stunned by her memory. If she could remember this, she told herself, she could remember the rest.

She stood on shaky legs and crossed the empty room for the desk that served as Zue's nursing station. A glass-fronted cabinet behind the chair held bandages and tape.

Her mind on her discovery, her nerves ringing, Lauren didn't see the shadow standing at the door of the clinic until it was too late. The door squeaked open and she jerked her head toward the sound, almost losing her balance in the process. Armando stood on the threshold.

"You're bleeding!" He came to her side in three long strides and took her hands in his. "What happened?"

They were inches apart and Lauren could feel the energy that seemed to be part of the air whenever Armando was near. Without waiting for an answer, he pulled her closer to the desk and opened the cabinet she'd been approaching.

"I—I had a dream," she stuttered. "When I woke up, I had scraped my hands on the railing—"

"I can see that." He began to clean her palms with a strong antiseptic, his movements swift and efficient, but kind at the same time. "Is that why you screamed?"

Still holding her hands, he turned from her to pick up the clean dressings, and Lauren realized she had a decision to make. She had to reconcile the disparate ways she felt about Armando and she had to do so quickly.

She made her decision impulsively.

"I've begun to get some of my memory back," she said. "I think I know how I ended up in the river."

ARMANDO WENT QUIET, Lauren's statement freezing him. "Tell me," he said.

She licked her lips and briefly told him

her dream. As she explained about the bridge, an uneasiness built inside him he didn't like. He knew the crossing she described and he'd heard nothing about that particular bridge being down. In fact, once a year, Manco made sure it was replaced so accidents like that wouldn't happen.

"Are you quite sure the rope went slack and *then* you fell?"

"Absolutely, yes. I'm positive."

He returned to tending her palms, his attitude as neutral as he could make it. He'd had a lot of questions about Lauren's presence from the very beginning, but what had really happened to her was near the top of the list.

He tied off the bandage, his voice noncommittal. "If the rope gave way, I'd say it was frayed then, wouldn't you?"

"Not necessarily. Someone could have worked on it before I got there and weakened the twine. My weight in the center would have been enough to get the job done."

Armando hid his surprise at her astuteness. "But why would anyone do such a thing? Do you think someone's out to hurt you?"

"No, I don't think that, but who knows? I ended up in that river and I want to know why."

He put a final piece of tape in place, then released her, replacing the tools and antiseptic in the cabinet behind them. "You need to get back into bed."

She didn't move. "I want to go see it."

He knew what she meant but he asked the question anyway, giving himself some time to think. "See what?"

"The bridge," she answered impatiently. "I want to go back there. I might remember more once I see it."

"It's a half-day hike from here. You don't have the strength."

Her jaw tightened, a look of determination adding to the frown she already wore. "I might not have it today," she said, "but I will soon. And when I do, I'm going back."

"Do you think that's wise?"

"I don't know if it's wise or not," she snapped. "But I don't have a choice in the matter. If I want to figure out what happened to me, I have to go back to that bridge."

LAUREN PROCEEDED TO DO exactly as she'd promised Armando. She choked down every drop of soup Zue brought her and swallowed every pill without comment. Three times a day, she walked an ever-widening circle around the clinic's compound. In a week, she felt much better, in two she was ready to hike.

The clinic was especially busy that Friday, a steady stream of patients coming in from all directions. She waited impatiently until the last one left, then she went into Armando's office with determination.

"I want to go see the bridge tomorrow," she announced. "I'm ready."

He put down the pen he'd been using to make notes on a chart and looked up at her, pushing his chair back from the desk at the same time. His eyes were speculative but they often were. She'd come to see that Armando accepted very little in the way of information without further examination.

"What makes you think you can make it?" he asked.

She was prepared. "I can walk four miles without tiring, nothing hurts and I've gained five pounds. My recovery time is over."

"Are you getting anxious to go home? I would expect you to care more about that rather than going back to the scene of the crime, as it were."

She tried to figure out how to answer as she sat down in the chair in front of his desk, one of Zue's wide, colorful skirts—all she had to wear—pooling around her feet. She'd had several conversations with her father since the initial one and his message had not changed. He wanted her to return to Dallas as soon as possible. But she didn't want that.

"My father has asked me that same question, numerous times as a matter of fact."

"And?"

"And I don't know. I guess I *should* want to go home but…"

He seemed to read her mind. "But you feel no urgent need."

She met his steady stare. "That's awful of me, isn't it?" she asked. "He's clearly worried and upset. I need to reassure him, but I feel like there are more answers for me *here* than there are back in Dallas."

Armando came from behind his desk to perch on the edge. "Why do you think that is the case?"

"You're the shrink," she said. "Why don't you tell me?"

"I should never have let you see my diploma," he said with a roll of his eyes.

"Maybe," she agreed. "You know my father is one, too."

"I know," he said.

"Don't you find that weird?" she asked. "That you're both psychiatrists?"

"Not really," he said with an engaging smile. "There *are* quite a few of us, you know. We're not a rare breed."

"It just seems strange to me," she said. "I don't believe in coincidences."

"How do you know?" he asked softly.

She blinked in surprise, then said, "I just do."

"You're remembering more and more," he noted. "That is good."

"I guess it is," she agreed, "but it's like putting a giant jigsaw puzzle together. I remember I like purple, but what shade? I know I lived in Peru as a child, but I can't recall our home. The pieces are all there but they don't quite fit."

"They will eventually."

"I don't intend to wait for 'eventually.'" She stood and they were eye to eye. A shiver she wasn't expecting went down her back at their nearness. She pushed its appearance aside and concentrated on the moment at hand. "Visiting the bridge will speed things up."

"I do not believe you are ready. Your strength is much better but traveling to where the bridge is located..." He shook his head. "I don't know."

"Well, I do," she said stubbornly. "I've been exercising and I want to go. If you won't take me, then I'll find a way to get there on my own."

Their gazes met and this time the impact

was even more noticeable. Armando wasn't a man who could be ignored but Lauren couldn't allow physical attraction to dictate her actions.

"You are a very stubborn woman," he said.

She looked at him unblinkingly. "Will you take me?"

He gave a Latin sigh, then spoke with resigned acquiescence. "All right. You win. We will go in the morning. Wear pants and bring a sweater."

ARMANDO CALLED MEREDITH that night on his encrypted cell phone and told her about the upcoming trek. She quizzed him about Lauren, asking why she simply didn't come home now that she knew her true identity.

He repeated Lauren's comment.

"What does that mean?" Meredith demanded. "Why would she feel there are 'more answers' for her in Peru? Answers to what?"

Armando spoke with uncharacteristic hesitation. "I'm not sure. She said something else that concerned me even more."

"And that was?"

"She said she didn't believe in coincidences."

"So?"

"I think she came here for a reason, Meredith. I have a feeling her magazine article was just a cover for something else."

"And *I* think you must be getting paranoid on me."

"Maybe," he conceded, "but I agree with her. I don't believe in coincidences, either. She did not come to Peru just to wander about the ruins and write some pretty essay." He'd given the facts a lot of thought and he'd decided there was only one real reason for her appearance. He told Meredith that reason now. "We'd be foolish to think her mother's death has nothing to do with her trip here."

Meredith's pause echoed down the line, her voice puzzled when she spoke. "You don't think she suspects you had anything to do with that, do you? Wasn't she shot by an intruder?"

"That was what the embassy's press release said but I always wondered. My gut feeling told me something else went on there that night."

"But how could Lauren have been involved? She was…what? Ten years old?"

Armando closed his eyes but the image in his brain didn't go away. "She was ten. Officials in the States believed there was a mole inside the Peruvian embassy and they thought Margaret Stanley might be it. I was sent there to eliminate her." He paused until his pulse steadied. "But I arrived too late. She was already dead, supposedly killed by a burglar. No one was ever arrested and eventually the matter was dropped. The press moved on to its next tragedy."

"That's convenient. *Was* Margaret Stanley the mole?"

"The problems at the embassy stopped after her death, so it was assumed so," he answered. "The father took Lauren and departed the country right after Margaret's death. I had developed a contact on the inside, but he had no idea who I really was, of course. I couldn't call him up afterward and ask."

"Who was he?"

"His name was Daniel Cunningham. He was Margaret's attaché. I arranged to play squash beside his court one day and we struck up a conversation. He invited me to the embassy's Christmas party and that's how I gained access."

"Who do *you* think killed her? And why cover it up?"

"Why is any crime covered up? To hide another one, I would presume. As to who actually pulled the trigger, I don't know, although I always wondered about the father."

"He is a nervous fellow, kinda strange." Meredith's voice lightened. "Then again, he *is* a psychiatrist. You guys are all pretty weird."

"Cunningham had said the man was little more than a fixture but Stanley definitely had the motivation if he'd wanted to kill her. He was very unhappy. He didn't want to be in Peru and I could understand why. He'd had a large practice back in the States and he'd sacrificed it to come with his wife."

"Could he have been the mole?"

Everything had pointed to J. Freeman Stanley as the guilty party, but to Armando that fact alone was enough to make him suspicious of any conclusion. "I wondered about that, too," Armando replied, "but no one wanted my opinion on the matter. I was only the hired help."

Promising Meredith another report when he had more to tell her, Armando hung up a few minutes later.

Lauren was waiting early the next morning, a backpack at her feet, when he stepped outside his bungalow. Gazing out over the valley beyond the clinic, she seemed unaware of his presence until he crossed the grass that separated them. As she turned at his approach, Armando hoped, just as he had sixteen years previously, that her father hadn't been involved with her mother's murder. To a child, a loss like that was overwhelming. A betrayal on top of it would be impossible to accept, even after all these years.

He put aside his concerns, his attention diverted by her clothing.

She'd dressed as he'd instructed but something didn't seem right about her pants.

Seeing his puzzled expression, she tugged on one baggy leg. "Recognize them?"

He frowned and looked closer, then raised his eyes to hers. "Are those mine?"

She grinned. "Zue stole them for me. I didn't have anything else."

"They fit you a lot differently than they fit me."

"Thank goodness they do," she said. "If they didn't, I'd be worried."

He started to argue. If she hadn't looked so great, he wouldn't have been quite as distracted as he now found himself. Forcing his eyes away from her curves, he tried to concentrate on the upcoming task. "Are you ready to go?"

"Yes." She set her tea cup and saucer on the nearby patio table. "I've been up since daylight. I guess I'm nervous."

"You might be in for an unpleasant time," he warned. "Do you understand?"

"I do," she said, "but it doesn't matter. I *need* to see."

He hadn't expected to convince her otherwise, but he'd had to try. "All right, then. Let's go."

She grabbed her bag and they set off toward the barn. He'd told Zue last night to see that the BMW was ready and the tank topped off, and as always, she'd followed his instructions to the letter. Leaning just inside the opened doors, the bike was ready, the bags packed with water bottles and food.

Behind him, Lauren stopped. "Hey! I thought you said we had to hike—"

"I said it *was* a half-day hike. I didn't say we had to go that way."

"That's not fair!"

"Life *isn't* fair here. We could break down, we could have an accident, we could be ambushed…a million things could happen to us, all of them bad. If you didn't have the strength to walk out on your own, then you weren't prepared. I don't operate that way."

He expected her to argue, but her gaze

narrowed and she stared at him instead. "You're right," she conceded. "I wasn't thinking straight."

He nodded once, then threw one leg over the seat. She joined him, and a moment later, they headed for the jungle.

LAUREN WOULD HAVE CUT OUT her tongue before she complained but she was definitely relieved when Armando slowed the powerful cycle. For more than an hour, they'd been riding over what was basically a path, and she was ready to take a break. Every rut and bump had made itself known and she was aching in ways she'd never before experienced. Even worse than the roughness of the ride, however, was the impact of Armando's nearness. She wasn't accustomed to the sensations he was creating within her and she didn't know how to deal with them.

He came to a stop then eased off the trail, parking the motorcycle in the underbrush. Lauren's ears rang with the silence, a sweep of vertigo hitting her as Armando got off the motorcycle and removed his helmet.

"Are you all right?" Before she could answer, he took her hand, turning it over and placing two of his broad fingers over her pulse point by her wrist. "You look pale."

"I'm fine." She tried to tug her hand away but he tightened his grip and sent her a look of warning that stilled her. A current flowed from his fingertips up her arm and into her chest.

Dropping his fingers a second later, he shook his head. "You need to take it easy for just a bit. I don't like your heart rate going up that high. We'll rest here and get something to eat before we walk in." He tilted his head to indicate the jungle behind them. "The bridge is just over that rise."

She looked in the direction he indicated and frowned. Nothing around them seemed familiar. "Are you sure?"

"The jungle can change over the course of a single hour. Unless you were raised here, you cannot tell the difference from one spot to another."

"But you do," she pointed out.

"My life depends on it. Everyone else needs a guide…."

He answered her with distraction, then jerked his eyes to Lauren's face. "Wait! Who *was* your guide?" he asked. "You must have had one."

The question triggered a chain reaction and Lauren's mouth fell open as the memory came to her.

"I did!" she agreed in obvious shock. "But I can't remember…." A name hovered on the very tip of her tongue, then it flitted away like one of the butterflies overhead. A second later, she grabbed it. "His name was Joaquin Peña!" she said in excitement. "I found him when I went to the train station in Cuzco. Do you know him? He said he lived in Rojo. There can't be that many guides."

A shadow passed over Armando's expression. "I'm not sure," he seemed to hedge.

"He said Rojo was near the ruins and he knew the area well. I hired him and…" She licked her lips and frowned, the memory coming back slowly. "He left me!" she said, her eyes going round. "I was crossing the bridge and I turned to look and he was gone." She blinked as she remembered her fear, her mind reeling with the sudden list of possibilities that came to her.

"That's very strange." Armando frowned. "He didn't let anyone know what had happened."

"Why not?"

"That is a very good question," he answered. "I wonder why myself."

He seemed to think about it some more, then he clearly dismissed the problem, turning instead to the saddlebags on the motorcycle. Unloading bottles of water, sandwiches and fruit, he handed one of each to her. "We're not going further until we eat."

Lauren did as he instructed, but she tasted nothing, and the minute she was finished, she jumped up from the tarp he'd spread out for them to sit on. "I'm ready," she announced. "Let's go!"

He put away their things with maddening slowness, then shocked her by pulling out a machete from a leather holster. Seeing her look of horror at the knife, he explained, "There are snakes out here, Lauren. The kind that slither on the ground *and* the kind that walk on two legs." He ran his thumb down the blade. "I can use this on the underbrush and them as well, if need be."

Lauren stared at the instrument and hoped it wouldn't be necessary, at least not beyond cutting through the jungle.

He set off into the thicket, the machete slicing through the greenery with scary ease. She scrambled to catch up. There was a path, she realized, but if Armando had not been leading the way, she wouldn't have seen it.

They walked for ten minutes, and the sounds that assailed them—the bird calls, the monkey howls, the unexplainable rustles in the brush—seemed unreal. She was glad Armando was with her. The noise was bad enough on its own, but within minutes, when the greenery pushed closer and the smells grew stronger, she turned even more grateful. A looming sense of fear compressed the air around her and panic rose within her. With Armando one step ahead of her, Lauren fought against the sensation, but she was beginning to lose ground when Armando stopped and moved to one side.

Sweating and anxious, she halted, too, her eyes following his outstretched hand. In the clearing that lay before them, there were two cliffs overflowing with growth, separated by a deep gorge. From the depths of the seemingly bottomless space came the sound of rushing water.

"This is it." Armando tilted his head toward the narrow canyon. "The Xuachoto River is down there and the bridge is just past that big rubber tree."

Lauren wiped her brow across her sleeve and pretended she was fine. "It isn't there anymore, and I'm here to testify to that."

His gaze held no judgment. "Then let's go see," was all he said.

He hacked at leaves and vines for another few yards, then he stopped again just as Lauren took a final breath and pressed forward. She almost crashed into him, but it wasn't his body that stopped her; it was his expression. Despite the jungle heat, her breath froze before she even understood why.

"What is it?" Her voice held a tremor.

Instead of speaking, he motioned her to stand beside him, but Lauren couldn't move. After pushing him so hard to bring her to the bridge, she couldn't believe it, but she didn't want to take another step. She knew she had to, though, and she forced her feet to move.

He lifted the machete and pointed. Lauren followed the razor-sharp edge with her eyes.

Stretching across the gorge, a rope bridge swayed slowly in the hot morning sun. A platform of rough planks approached it and knots as big as apples secured it to two mahogany trees. As Lauren stared, a macaw swooped down and perched on one of the twisting handrails, his weight increasing the bridge's motion. The bird's cry split the air with a resonance that echoed in the fecund silence. His scorn seemed to be directed straight at Lauren.

The bridge looked as if it'd been there from the beginning of time and never been touched.

CHAPTER FOUR

LAUREN CLOSED HER EYES momentarily, then she opened them, again, their sapphire depths shockingly blue as she turned to him. "It fell. I was on it. Someone has obviously replaced it since then."

"That isn't possible," he said flatly. "The locals work for months on those things. One side alone could take at least eight weeks, probably more. They make them in the winter when there's nothing else to do."

Her comment made him think of Joaquin Peña. He wasn't anything, much less a guide. He spent his days thinking up ways to make money without working while chewing coca leaves with his friends, one of whom was Zue's grandson, Beli.

Zue tried to keep the boy away from the gang, but she usually failed. One thing Joaquin hadn't lied about was the name of his village. He *was* from Rojo.

Lauren hadn't just "found" him when she'd arrived at the station. He never left home because it was too much trouble. If he'd gone to Cuzco, it was for the sole purpose of looking for her.

Why?

She stepped onto the platform and nodded toward the ropes. "Are there spares sitting around?"

Uneasy with her proximity to the edge, Armando came to where she stood. "Generally Peruvians don't believe in being prepared, but Manco is the exception. He replaces the bridges almost every year. He could have had one ready to go." He shifted his eyes to hers. "But if he'd strung a fresh one, he would have told us."

"Are you sure?" Her voice was full of suspicion.

"No. Nothing is for certain in Peru. Especially when it's this important. Attempted murder is a serious thing."

The minute the phrase left his lips, Armando regretted his choice of words, but it was too late to take them back. Lauren's throat moved as she swallowed nervously. "Attempted murder? Is that what you think this was?"

"You said yourself you don't believe in coincidences. I don't think your guide just decided to return home at the exact time you say the bridge decided to fray and break, do you?"

She shook her head slowly. "No, I don't."

"Then you have a problem." Armando's voice was soft but couldn't ease the tension within her.

Her eyes went back to the bridge. "I'd say I do," she agreed. "But why?"

"You're asking the wrong person." Armando paused and her gaze came back to his. "*You* are the only one who can answer that question."

THE RIDE BACK TO THE CLINIC seemed to take forever. When they pulled into the compound's gate, Lauren wasn't sure she could lift her leg over the motorcycle and climb off. Stiff, sore, confused and upset... There were plenty of adjectives she could have used to describe herself, but she concentrated on a detail that had been bothering her instead—the look she'd seen on Armando's face when she'd named the man who'd been her guide.

She stayed on the motorcycle and watched him climb off. "I have to ask you something."

Armando pulled off his helmet, took one look at her, then began to shake his head. "No questions. You're exhausted. I did what you wanted, now you must do what I want. Rest."

"Just answer this and I won't ask for another thing, I promise."

"I doubt that," he said with exaggerated patience, "but I have a feeling you're going to ask regardless."

She didn't make a liar of him. "You

know the man who took me to the bridge, don't you? Joaquin Peña? You recognized his name."

He seemed to consider his answer for a moment, then he spoke. "Yes. I know Joaquin. Let's just say he is not someone you should have chosen to guide you."

"Why is that?"

"He's worthless," Armando said bluntly. "He hangs around with Zue's grandson and does nothing productive. He has no job, no responsibilities and spends most of his time looking for ways to get money that don't involve work."

Lauren chuckled, albeit uneasily. "He sounds like a lot of rich men I've met."

"Joaquin isn't rich. And he definitely isn't a guide."

Her expression turned wary. "Why would he come to me and say that he was?"

"I don't know. Maybe that's something we should find out."

Nodding her agreement, she started to dismount, then winced in pain. A loud "ouch…" escaped and she sat back down, any other questions she might have had fleeing her mind.

Armando was instantly at her side and shaking his head. "I should not have let you convince me you were ready. This is my fault."

Using her hands, she lifted her left leg over the saddle and gave another groan. "You couldn't resist my womanly wiles," she answered, trying to lighten the moment. "Don't blame yourself. You didn't have a chance."

"I'll admit that could be true." His eyes lingered on hers long enough to bring an unexpected heat to her face. "You seem to have some ability in that department."

To cover her blush, she started to stand but found she couldn't. Her legs went out from under her, and if Armando hadn't caught her, she would have ended up in the dirt.

Instead, she ended up in his arms.

Their faces were an inch apart. "Let me help you," he said.

"I think you already have."

After a long moment passed, they pulled

back at the same time. The damage had already been done, though. Lauren felt as if she'd been electrified, the power of his touch rippling through her entire body. Keeping his grip at her waist, Armando steadied her, and walking slowly, they crossed the grassy area between the barn and the clinic.

He didn't release her until they reached her bed. Lowering her carefully, Armando straightened, then looked down at her. "I want you to rest," he said sternly. "We set you back with this trip."

She gripped the railing at the edge of the bed as relief washed over her. She wasn't sure if it came from the fact that she'd made it to the bed or if she was happy to be away from the heat of Armando's body. She decided it was the latter.

"I had to go," she said resolutely. "I had to see that bridge."

"And now?"

"Now I have even more questions than I did before. And there aren't any answers in sight."

IN THE DAYS THAT FOLLOWED, her dreams got worse.

The blond man appeared over and over, and each time he held a gun. It was always aimed at the bridge where she stood, but when he fired, sometimes a bullet came and sometimes a streak of red shot from the barrel instead.

The first night that happened, Lauren woke with a scream in her throat, her hands held protectively in front of her face.

The next night, the dream came again. This time a condor was on the platform beside her.

The third night, Armando held the gun.

When she woke up the fourth night, her memory had returned.

She instantly wished it hadn't.

IT WAS CLOSE TO MIDNIGHT when Armando finally sat down at his computer to e-mail Meredith. An outbreak of flu had kept him busy all week but he'd finally found the time to talk to Manco that morning about the bridge. Their conversation had left Armando puzzled, to say the least.

According to the tribal leader, the bridge had been in perfect shape when his people had located Lauren. He'd been shocked at the idea of the rope being frayed. "I keep them in perfect condition," he'd stated imperially. "Nothing was wrong with that bridge. I would not allow it." Armando had considered asking to speak to the men who had actually rescued Lauren, but decided against it. The trouble a request like that would cause wouldn't be worth the effort. They would back Manco, regardless.

Armando's fingers tapped the keys with precision.

L. insisted on returning to the bridge last week but when we arrived, everything was fine. The ropes were intact and nothing had been disturbed. I'm not sure how this was accomplished...or if it even was. I spoke with the local village leader and he said the bridge had never been down.

What kind of maladaptive behaviors

bothered Lauren following her mother's death? How severe were they? Do they still persist?

He sent the message with a click of his mouse, then he pivoted his chair and leaned back, his gaze going, as it always did, to the emptiness outside his window. He made his mind just as blank, forcing the thoughts and worries of the day into oblivion. He'd practiced meditation for years, but he'd gotten better after arriving in Peru. If he'd been a mystic, he might have attributed his growing ability to his proximity to Machu Picchu; since he wasn't, he couldn't really explain why he'd improved.

Ten minutes later, a soft *ding* brought him back.

He twisted his chair to face the computer screen again, taking a sip of the now tepid tea he'd brought with him earlier. A small envelope icon flashed at the bottom of his screen.

Don't know what to tell you, Meredith had written. Stanley said she'd suffered depression as a teenager, apparently severe enough to warrant hospitalization. Says she's fine now but he worried about her for so long, he found the habit hard to break. Also said they were very close. He threw out a couple of psych terms but they were gobbledygook to me. Should I call him for more info?

Armando typed quickly. Not yet. I'll be in touch and then... Concentrating on what he wanted to say next, he stared at the screen and focused, his thoughts running ahead of his brain.

When a voice spoke behind him, he reacted without thinking.

ONE MOMENT HE WAS AT HIS DESK typing and, in the next, he was at her side. Lauren froze, her back pressed against Armando's chest, one of his arms at her waist, the other one across her throat. She could breathe but just barely, her fright stealing the air from her lungs more than Armando's hold. Her amnesia had stripped her of memories but it had also shielded her from

her fears. Now that she'd remembered everything, she had nothing left to protect
her.

"I—I didn't mean to startle you," she
said, her mouth dry. "Am I interrupting
something?"

He cursed and yanked his arm away.
"God, Lauren, I'm sorry! I was not expecting anyone…. But then I guess that is
obvious, no?"

Staring at him, Lauren raised her hand
and massaged her throat. He'd reacted much
too quickly and way too smoothly for a
doctor, but she suspected she knew why.

"Exactly what kind of psychiatrist did
you say you are?" she joked anyway. "The
shrinks I've known generally can't walk
and chew gum at the same time, much less
move that quickly."

"I didn't say."

Lauren waited but the awkward silence
only grew; he wasn't going to answer her
question and she wasn't surprised.

He resumed his seat at his desk and
motioned for her to sit on a nearby bench.

Moving his mouse with efficient quickness, he closed the window he'd had open on his computer, then turned his chair to face her. He hadn't wanted her to see whatever was on the screen.

"What brings you out this time of night?" His eyes swept over the frilly robe Zue had loaned her.

She pulled the thin material closer. "I think I need to talk to you."

"This sounds important."

He smiled as he spoke, but there were lines of weariness around his eyes and shadows in the hollows of his cheekbones. She'd seen the crowded clinic and knew how busy he'd been.

"I've been having that dream again," she said. "The one I told you about earlier."

"Where you're on the bridge?"

"Yes." She formed her reply carefully. "I've had variations of it since I got here but I didn't understand completely until tonight. Seeing the bridge must have triggered something for me."

Lauren told herself she was being silly,

but it seemed as if he tensed. His voice was steady when he spoke, however. "Go on."

"I'm crossing the rope bridge and a man appears on the other side, a blond man. He had a gun and he shoots the rope. It breaks and I fall."

"Then what happens?" he asked blandly.

"Then I wake up," she said.

Picking up a paper clip from his desk, he unfolded the wire without looking at it. "And this dream has told you something that it hadn't the last time you experienced it?"

"Yes, it has," she confirmed. "It changed slightly each night but each change told me more. Finally, I remembered…everything."

He studied her, and Lauren found herself holding her breath, the clock on his desk ticking loudly in the silence.

"I know who you are," she said in a quiet voice. "And I know what you do."

CHAPTER FIVE

ARMANDO WENT COLD. WHAT was Lauren saying? Did she remember seeing him the night of her mother's death?

"I don't believe I understand," he said. "What exactly do you mean?"

"You know what I mean," she replied. "You've been hiding here for years, hoping no one would figure out your real identity."

A series of possibilities flashed through his mind.

He could lie to her.

He could deny her accusation.

He could kill her.

She leaned closer, her elbows on her knees, her eyes too intense to ignore. "I know who you are, Dr. Torres-*Bernuy*. You aren't a simple doctor or even 'just' a psychiatrist. You're famous. And you interpret dreams and memories like no one else has ever been able to do."

Armando couldn't help himself. He got up, his overwhelming relief too turbulent to control while sitting down. She thought she'd uncovered his darkest secret, but she had no idea. No idea at all.

"I figured this out over a year ago and I started planning my trip back then." Lauren stood, too. "I came to Peru just to meet you. I've had recurring nightmares since I was a child."

"Out of the air, you plucked my name? What made you think I could help—"

"My father's a psychiatrist," she reminded him. "He had articles about you in his library. I knew you had to be the best at what you do if he was impressed enough to read about you."

Freeman Stanley knew about his earlier work? Doctors of Stanley's stature rarely concerned themselves with the studies of those younger and less experienced, especially from different countries. Armando masked his surprise with a show of anger. "So you tracked me down like some kind of big-game hunter? Why did you do this? Who do you think you are to invade my privacy like that?"

She crossed the space between them and looked up at him, her eyes pleading with him to understand. "I need you to explain things to me." She put her hand on his arm. "I *had* to come see you."

"I no longer work with dreams. You've wasted your time."

"But you can help me!" she said. "I know you—"

"I don't believe in dream interpretation anymore because dreams are meaningless," he lied outright, "and memories can change. Anyone who thinks otherwise is misguided. I have nothing to do with that now."

"Why?"

"I don't have to tell you why," he replied coldly. "All you need to know is that you will not find what you seek here. If *that* is the only reason you came to Peru, you should turn around immediately and go back to Texas."

"Can't you make an exception?"

He stared at her stonily.

"I know you're a good man."

Her expression shifted and he could see how much this meant to her, but helping Lauren recover her past was not something he could ever do.

"How can you refuse me?"

"It's simple. All I do is say 'no.'" Hardening himself to her plight, he pointed behind her to the doorway. "Please leave me now. You've disturbed my peace enough for one night."

She waited so long he thought he might have to physically escort her out, but she did turn and walk toward the door. Once there she paused. "You have a skill no one else has or even understands," she said. "It's a sin to waste it."

"I've committed many sins in my lifetime." He smiled at her naiveté. "Ignoring this ability would be the least of them, I promise you."

"I'm not leaving here without learning the truth."

His voice went flat. "Then you're going to be in Peru for a very long time."

He returned to the computer and, a moment later, he heard the door close behind her. Glancing over his shoulder to make sure she was gone, he shut down his machine, this latest turn of events something he hadn't anticipated at all.

He kept a bottle of Scotch in his desk and, reaching for it now, Armando poured himself a drink, the memories pricking him, their barbs as sharp as ever.

He'd been a young medical student when his ability to decipher dreams had begun to get him noticed. With patient after patient, he realized he could understand what motivated them if they described their visions to him. Working with dreams was nothing new in his field, but Armando seemed to have a special gift. After a bit, his patients began to compare notes and before he could stop it, his reputation grew. His father, a noted Argentinian psychiatrist, encouraged him to take advantage of the financial possibilities but Armando had been repelled by the idea, just as he was repelled by most of his wealthy father's advice.

The defiant younger son, Armando had already been at odds with his family. Unlike the elder Dr. Torres, Armando couldn't ignore the unfair economics of a country filled with corruption. Dictators and killers, thieves and con artists, the so-called leaders of Argentina had everything but they gave nothing back to the people. They took advantage of the uneducated and underprivileged on a continual basis.

Armando joined the underground movement dedicated to changing the government but, in truth, the organization had no power. By the time Meredith's father called him, he was ready to move on. The Operatives appealed to him immediately and his experience made him a valuable member of the team. No one ever knew his role in a situation until it was too late. Cardiac arrest, lung failure, kidney disease.

The deaths had always been labeled natural.

Only Armando knew better.

If she thought she could make Armando return to his father's world, then Lauren Stanley really was crazy. In every sense of the word.

UPSET AND ANXIOUS, Lauren walked back to the hospital through the darkness. The lack of light should have bothered her but it seemed comforting instead. If no one could see her, she could pretend she didn't exist and, if she didn't exist, then neither did her problems. She had the thought, then laughed out loud at her foolish logic.

Things didn't actually work that way and she knew it.

She crossed the clearing and faced the truth. Her problems remained, and it seemed at this moment as if they always would. Armando had been her last hope. If he wouldn't help her, she was lost.

As soon as they'd returned from the bridge and the dreams had begun again,

Lauren's memories and mind had begun clearing. When she'd woken that morning, it'd almost felt as if her amnesia had never existed. She'd simply opened her eyes and everything had been there, including the awful time after her mom's suicide.

She'd even remembered the label she'd put on that part of her life, calling it the Missing Years. She'd missed a lot of experiences back then—her first slumber party, her first high-school dance, her first boyfriend. Mainly, however, she'd lost herself. From the time they'd returned to the States to midway through college, she hadn't really been present. A thick fog of depression had separated her from everyone else. She'd been too lethargic to try and escape, too young to try and explain.

When she'd gone to see Armando, she'd left the window by her bed open and the room had grown cold. She went to close it, but stopped her hands on the sash as she stared outside. Armando's cabin was easy to pick out. It was the only one still lit.

Her father hadn't wanted her to visit the country where her mother had lost her life but Lauren had been determined to return to Peru. He'd said she had gotten closure and to dig it all up again would be too painful.

But she'd already spotted the journals about Dr. Bernuy in his office. There had been a black-and-white photograph of Armando in the report and the minute she'd seen it, she'd been drawn to him. She'd put her research skills to work and she'd located him, convincing her boss to send her to Machu Picchu on assignment.

The irony struck her anew, but she didn't laugh. No one except Lauren herself had known her true reason for coming to Peru, but after the accident, she'd forgotten why she'd come.

She shook her head and cursed with disappointment. Armando had been her last hope at pushing aside her past and getting on with her life. She'd begun to put things in perspective as she'd gotten older but there had still been some niggling doubts because of her dreams and she'd felt he could put them all to rest. Now that wasn't going to happen.

He not only didn't want to help her, he wanted her gone. She closed her eyes as her hand went to the spot on her neck where he'd pressed his arm. She'd been shocked by his quickness.

But not completely.

His silence about his past, his caution, his quickness… The details formed a picture that matched the rumors she'd learned about him during her research. An article she'd found in an Argentinian social column in a Buenos Aires newspaper came to mind.

The son of a prominent local psychiatrist has once again disappeared from our lovely parties. Where does this Porteño, *one of our most eligible bachelors, go? Where does he fly away to, so quickly, like* El Condor?

The reference had astonished her, although she had no idea if it was deliberate or not. Operation Condor had been a collaborative project between several South American militaries and the United States. She'd written an article for *Luxury* about Buenos Aires and had uncovered a reference to the scheme while doing her background work. It had been a death call for leaders who weren't following the dictates of the men at the top. According to some, assassins, trained by the U.S. government, had been used.

She'd found more allusions to a dangerous life but none of them had been as obvious as this one.

Was Armando a killer as well as a doctor?

It sounded impossible, but this was Peru. Where the most bizarre was not only possible but probable.

The contradictions couldn't be ignored.

The man she'd come to know over the past few weeks was a caring, sympathetic physician who'd gained her immediate trust. He'd been kind and gentle, and she'd responded to him strongly, his sensuality another factor that had pulled her closer every day.

The magnetism she'd sensed in his photograph was even more powerful in person and now that she knew him better, she understood his appeal, but her feelings weren't that simple. She'd been attracted to him despite the rumors and now that she remembered them, she didn't care. What was going on with her?

She climbed into the bed and closed her eyes without expecting sleep to come, but it not only came, it came swiftly and hit her hard. In one moment, she was ten years old again and hiding in her mother's closet.

The action replayed itself like a movie being rewound. Her mother was lying on the floor, her beaded gown sparkling in the bathroom's lighting. A bright red rose lay on the carpet near her head.

A crow flew into the room. His black feathers held a wicked gleam, his eyes glinted with yellow light and a white collar circled his neck. To her, he represented the priest who'd later presided over her mother's covered casket. He'd been young and confused, the service a disjointed affair and awkward.

The bird hopped to her mother's body and grabbed the flower. It then reached to remove something else, using its beak this time instead of its claws. She thought it was a piece of gold jewelry but she wasn't sure why she thought that. Her mother had only worn platinum. A second later, the bird magically transformed into a small furry animal and scurried away, leaving Lauren alone until her father appeared. He ignored her and a feeling of abandonment came over her. She began to sob but her tears were silent.

No one could hear her.

The dream continued from there, any sense she could have made of it dissolving like a fine mist. Flashes of brightness, a brown face, a blond man, the sound of music…and then the gun. The images plagued her for hours, repeating themselves over and over. When she finally woke up the next morning, her cheeks were wet.

She'd cried all night.

WITHOUT TELLING LAUREN, Armando slipped away early the following morning and headed for Rojo, promising Zue he'd be back in time for his afternoon clinic. After he and Lauren had returned from seeing the bridge, he'd found Beli and asked him about his useless friend, Joaquin, but Zue's grandson had shrugged and denied any knowledge of the situation. Armando felt Lauren should go home as soon as possible, but he had to know what Joaquin was up to—if he'd had anything to do with that bridge going down, he needed to be held accountable.

He told himself that was his only reason for going to Rojo. He hadn't been moved by Lauren's pleas because he couldn't be. Finding the truth was all he cared about.

Hell. Who was he trying to kid?

Turning down her requests for help had stolen his sleep and kept him awake for hours. Lauren was a fascinating woman and despite his every intention, she was beginning to appeal to him on too many different levels to count.

He pulled into the village an hour later and headed straight for the school run by his friend, Ben Williamson. When it came to

Rojo, Williamson, a lay minister and the local teacher, knew everyone and everything.

Williamson threw open the scarred wooden door that led to the school's tiny office and greeted Armando before he could finish knocking. "Do my eyes deceive me or is it really *El Fantasmo*, the ghostly doctor?"

Williamson was a six-foot-four giant with flaming red hair and blue eyes as sharp as his tongue. He was an ex-Navy SEAL but he'd left the military to pursue his true calling—education. He'd started the facility in Rojo with funding from the church he'd belonged to back in the States, but he poured his heart and soul—as well as his own retirement funds—into it as well. The result was a mission school with a military flair. On Sundays, he preached, but he'd confessed to Armando once that he thought he intimidated more people into joining the church than he actually converted.

Armando endured the man's crushing hug and stepped into the cluttered office. "*El Fantasmo,* I don't know," he said. "Would you settle for a simple village doctor?"

Williamson fell into his creaky wooden desk chair and pointed Armando to the battered couch that leaned against the opposite wall. "There's nothing simple about you, Torres. Never try to shit a shitter."

Armando grinned, the man's earthy delivery a relief from the layers of innuendo that crowded every Peruvian exchange. "You're right," he said with a dip of his head. "You reign supreme in that category, Brother Williamson. I will grant you that truth."

Williamson made a blessing motion with his hand, acknowledging Armando's concession, but then his demeanor shifted and became more serious. "You've been a busy man," he said. "What the hell is this stuff that's going around? The flu?"

"Something like it." Armando shrugged. "It's not that bad."

"Half the parish used it as an excuse to stay home last Sunday," the redhead retorted. "Are you telling me they should have been in church?"

"I wouldn't presume to address their

spiritual needs," Armando replied. "I tend only to the body."

Williamson sent Armando a speculative look. "And from what I hear," he said, "you have quite a body out at the compound to tend to presently. A blonde, I believe? With blue eyes and a shapely figure?"

Armando wasn't surprised, but he acted as if he were. Part of their game involved letting Williamson shock him with his knowledge. "You know about the woman?" he said, lifting his eyebrows.

"I know everything." Williamson let the chair crash back to the floor. Placing his arms on the desk, he folded them and stared at Armando. "But tell me more."

Armando laughed. "Her name is Lauren Stanley. She's a writer from Dallas. Some of Manco's people fished her out of the river. She was injured by the fall, but she's doing better now."

"What the hell was she doing in that filthy ditch?"

Armando gave Williamson the details. "I still don't know what to think of it," he confessed. "But she said Joaquin Peña guided her there so I thought I'd drop in on him and see what he has to say about that."

Williamson's expression turned thoughtful. "If you want to contact Joaquin Peña, you're in for quite a journey."

Armando cursed. "I was afraid of this. He's disappeared, hasn't he?"

"Oh, no," Williamson replied. "I know right where he is. I prayed over him just yesterday. Right before they closed the casket."

"He's dead!"

"I hope so," Williamson replied. "We buried him."

"What happened?"

"I have no idea. The body was found behind his house. He'd supposedly been involved in a fight at the local cantina the night before, but who knows?" He raised a finger to his head and mimed a shooting motion, making the segue from teacher to SEAL in a single breath. "One bullet, close range—small caliber weapon, maybe a Koch 9. A clean kill. If it'd happened anywhere else I'd say it was a professional hit."

"No suspects?"

"Nope." Williamson shook his head. "But Peña wasn't a nice person. It wouldn't surprise me to find out he had something to do with that poor woman's problems."

They chatted for another half hour, then the bells began to ring outside the school.

Williamson jumped to his feet. "It's time for my afternoon class, Torres. Would you like to sit in and see what we do?"

"I'd love to, but my own work calls. Another time perhaps?" They shook hands, and the ex-SEAL offered a last bit of advice as Armando headed out the door.

"You might try and talk to Peña's brother," he suggested. "They lived together. I guess he's still residing in their humble abode." He jerked a thumb over his shoulder. "Up the hill, take a right, then a left. There's a lovely collection of underfed farm animals out front. You can't miss it."

WITH RED-STREAKED EYES and a headache that wouldn't quit, Lauren rose late and walked from the hospital to the bungalow that housed the kitchen. Zue laid out the compound's meals and let the families and the invalids who could walk help themselves. Only the sickest patients had their food delivered. As soon as Lauren had been able, she'd been expected to come to the long wooden table instead of eating in bed and she had. The others were accustomed to seeing her but when she walked inside close to noon, she sensed a tension that hadn't been present before.

She hesitated on the threshold, then, grabbing a small plate, she put fresh mango slices on one side and one of Zue's rolls on the other. With a mug of coffee, she made her way to the end of the table where she usually sat.

The Quechuan conversation she'd interrupted resumed, and Lauren listened as hard as she always did. She did this to help her learn the language but today the goal was one of pure distraction. If Armando wasn't going to help her, she had to come up with another plan. Considering the night she'd just had, the effort seemed overwhelming. Her dream hung over her head like a bleak cloud.

Someone at the far end of the table spoke, and Lauren focused, the man's tone catching her attention more than the conversation itself. He was obviously upset and close to tears. Lauren got *baby,* and *sick,* then he said something that hushed everyone, prompting several to lower their heads and move their lips in silent prayer.

When the talk resumed, Lauren asked Zue what was wrong. They'd developed an understanding of sorts, through a combination of Spanish, Quechuan and sign language.

It took several tries, but Lauren eventually understood. The man had come late that morning with a very sick child. Zue had tried to call Armando but so far he was out of range. The little boy had stopped breathing several times, Zue acted out, a wrinkled hand on her chest and then her nose. She wasn't sure if he would live or not.

The situation sounded too serious to simply ignore.

"Take me to see the child." Lauren made a walking motion with her hand then pointed to herself.

Zue shook her head, her expression stubborn. They argued briefly, then Lauren understood the older woman's rationalization. She was afraid Lauren might catch whatever the child had. Lauren prevailed and Zue finally gave in.

They headed for one of the buildings Lauren hadn't been in before. Walking inside, she realized Armando had prepared a special place just for his youngest patients, the beds smaller, the walls painted with bright jungle scenes. As spotless as the adults' clinic, this area was brighter and happier, with toys in one corner and a pint-size table and chairs in another. Lauren found herself fascinated by this unexpected revelation about Armando, but she gave it no more thought. Hurrying, she headed for the tiniest bed where a little boy lay on his stomach, his face toward the door.

He was barely breathing. His skin was a dusky shade of ash, his whole body limp and unmoving. Lauren glanced at Zue, who frowned, the boy's father hovering anxiously nearby. The child had gotten much worse, she communicated, in the past hour.

Lauren placed her hand on the boy's shoulder but he didn't move, even when she shook him gently. Fear came over her and waiting for Armando began to seem like a very bad option. She rolled the little boy over and tilted his head back, one hand on his forehead, the other on his chin. Her panic swelled when she put her ear against his mouth and nose. Only seconds before he'd been taking shallow breaths, but now he'd stopped breathing completely.

She had to do something and she had to do it fast.

With shaking fingers she pinched his nose and sealed his mouth with her own. Holding back an urge to fill his lungs, she puffed gently, delivering two slow but deliberate breaths. She paused and prayed, her hand on his bare chest. His rib cage didn't rise at all.

Frightened, Lauren tried again but got the same response. With no time to think, she put one hand on his chest and the other on top of it. She was on her fourth thrust when he started to gag and cough.

Just as Armando walked inside.

"YOU SAVED THAT CHILD'S LIFE." Armando stared across the dining-room table at Lauren, a pair of candles flickering between them over the remains of their dinner. He'd been impressed by her actions with the toddler. Her conduct had not been what he would have expected from a writer who told rich people where to travel and how to spend their money. "The boy's father thinks you're a *bruja blanca*."

"I'm not a witch." Lauren smiled. "It was pure luck."

"But white witches are good."

She pushed back from the table and picked up her plate. "If I hadn't taken a

Red Cross course, not so long ago, I wouldn't have had a clue about what to do."

"Well, you did take it and you knew what to do." He watched her carry her dishes to the sideboard and put them on the tray for Zue.

"You're giving me way too much credit, Armando."

"The shot of antibiotics will cure his congestion but if you hadn't gotten him breathing again, nothing would have mattered. That child survived, thanks to you."

"Whatever you say," she conceded. "I guess it's just too bad I can't wave my magic wand for myself."

Armando recognized the ploy for what it was, but this time he hesitated. The murder of Joaquin Peña had given him second thoughts about his decision not to help Lauren. It didn't seem likely the man had been killed as the result of a brawl. The circumstances described by Williamson just didn't seem to fit, although with the Peñas anything was possible. If his death *had* been associated with Lauren's accident, though, that presented an entirely different set of problems. When he got Zue's message, Armando had had to abandon his plans to talk with Peña's brother.

Lauren returned to the table and picked up his plate to put it on the tray with her own. When she came back for his wineglass, he stopped her, his fingers wrapping around her wrist. "I went to Rojo to talk to your guide, Lauren. I wanted to question him about the accident."

Her eyes went wide. "What did he say?"

"He said nothing," Armando answered. "He couldn't. He's dead."

"D-dead? Oh, my God!"

"I doubt God has anything to do with Sr. Peña now," Armando replied, remembering his friend's words.

"What happened to him?"

"He was shot." Armando stood and went to the sideboard to refill his wineglass. He held the bottle out to Lauren, but she declined, her expression dazed.

"By whom?"

"No one knows." He sipped his wine. "I was going to talk to his brother, but I didn't have a chance after I got Zue's message. I spoke with a friend of mine in town who said Peña had brawled with someone at the local bar beforehand but nothing's been established."

"Will the police—"

"There are no police in Rojo."

"Then what will happen?"

"What *will* happen has *already* happened. He's been buried and prayed over. That's it unless the police in Cuzco get bored and decide to come and investigate, if you'd call what they do investigating."

She sat down and shook her head with disbelief. A few moments trickled by, then Armando found himself behind her chair, his hand poised to touch the strands of hair that lay across her shoulders. He stopped when she spoke, her voice making him aware of what he'd been about to do.

"Life is measured so differently here,

isn't it?" Her back was to him and he couldn't see her face, but her voice sounded hoarse. "It comes and it goes so easily. Too easily."

"I couldn't argue with that."

She sat in silence another few minutes, then she spoke again. "I lost my mother when I was ten. My father told me about it the first time we talked, but I didn't actually remember what happened until the other night."

As if he had no knowledge of her mother, Armando made an appropriate sound of distress.

"It's one of the things I dream about," she said woodenly. "I'm in the closet where I was hiding when it happened and I'm too scared to make a sound. There's a rose by her head, a red rose, and a crow. He's leaning over her and checking her pulse then he steals the rose. He turns into another animal and runs off."

Her symbols were so obvious, Armando couldn't believe she didn't understand

them. Anyone could have explained them
to her. Anyone, that is, who knew the truth.
 Anyone like himself.

CHAPTER SIX

LAUREN GAZED AT ARMANDO through tear-glazed eyes. "I'm sorry. I know you didn't want to hear about my dream," she said, "but seeing that poor father today brought it all back again. Death makes you feel so helpless, especially when it's someone you love. No one should have to face that." She couldn't contain a shudder. "I know. I found my mother's body. That's one memory I wish I hadn't got back."

Armando's face reflected the shock she'd known it would. "I'm very sorry, Lauren." His hand came down to rest on her shoulder, its weight more comforting than she would have thought. "I had no idea that part of your dream was literal. Dying is not a pretty experience, is it?"

"No, but my mother didn't simply die—she killed herself."

Armando straightened at once, shock crossing his features. "She committed suicide? I—I had no idea…."

Except for Dr. Gladney and her father, Lauren had never discussed her mother's suicide with anyone and now she knew why. The dismay on Armando's face brought back her own grief and made her feel it all over again.

"She was one of the consuls in Lima and she did it the night of the Christmas party when I was ten. I was hiding in her closet for some reason I can't recall and I came out and found her. She was lying on the floor. I began to scream and my father rushed in. After that, I remember nothing."

Armando almost looked as if he didn't believe her.

"It's the truth," she said defensively. "I'm not making this up."

He recovered quickly, his face a mask once more. "I believe you, Lauren. I do not think you are lying. I'm simply stunned. What a horrible thing for a child to experience."

"It *was* terrible," she said. "The State Department didn't want anyone to know and my father went along with it because he didn't want her reputation sullied. He knew the press would have a field day with the fact that someone 'unstable' had been put into a position that important. They put out a press release saying she'd surprised a burglar and the matter was dropped. We moved back to Dallas and that was it." She looked at him. "I guess you can understand why I have nightmares."

He took the chair beside hers and sat down heavily. "You have this dream frequently?"

"The details differ from time to time but the topic never changes."

"The trigger for a recurring dream is usually something life-shattering. It's almost always present with PTSD." He stopped and started to explain. "Post-Traumatic—"

"Stress Disorder," she finished for him. "I know all the buzzwords and I know all the theories. What I don't know is how to resolve the problem."

"You feel you have no closure."

Her father had used that term and, hearing it again, she felt a rise of resentment. "I don't believe in 'closure.' When someone dies, they're gone and you aren't. That matter can't be closed."

"But you can learn to deal with the loss."

She smiled thinly. "As I have? By dreaming about it every night?"

"There are other ways."

They stared at each other in silence, then Lauren saw a flicker in Armando's eyes that made her want to try one more time. She came to where he sat and kneeled at his side, her hands on the arm of his chair.

"You could help me," she said. "All I need is an explanation of the dream and then I could put my past behind me. My psyche is trying to give me a message and I can't move on until I understand it. This is a warning sign that I need to deal with and not just keep pushing away."

"Where did you get that theory?" he

asked. "It sounds like it came off the Internet."

His sarcasm stung. "You're mocking me."

"I'm telling you the truth." He paused, then his eyes softened. "Nightmares don't foretell the future or carry secret meanings, Lauren. Dreaming about a black widow spider doesn't mean you're going to kill your lover the next day. It might just mean you saw a black spider the week before when you were cleaning out a closet. There's nothing magic about the symbols."

"Then where did your reputation come from?"

"Patients who knew no better." He stood and held out his hands to pull her to her feet. She took his fingers reluctantly and let him help her up. They were inches apart and her pulse quickened at the nearness of his body. Details registered with her that she hadn't noticed before now—the shine of his hair, the scent of his aftershave, the shadows beneath his eyes. He looked weary but it made him all the more appealing.

"They were ignorant people," he said

quietly. "You're an educated woman and you should know better. I have no mystical powers, Lauren."

"But you could help me," she repeated.

He shook his head. "There's only one person who can help you."

"That one person is you."

"No." He lifted his right hand and put it flatly on her chest, just below her throat and right above her breasts. He tapped his fingers once. "That person is *you. You* are the only one who can come to terms with the images that haunt you. You and you alone."

"But I don't know how."

His eyes filled with a detachment that made her shiver. "Then maybe that's the way it's supposed to be," he said. "Sometimes we're better off not knowing."

LAUREN'S REVELATIONS LEFT Armando concerned but he had no time to think about them the next day. As it was on every Saturday, the clinic was flooded with patients who had waited the entire week to come see him. In between the wailing children and upset mothers, he managed a few quiet moments to reflect on the surprise Lauren had given him. When she'd described the crow, he'd felt as if someone had put two paddles against his chest and turned on the current. But when she'd continued, his shock had given way to utter confusion.

Lauren thought her mother had killed herself.

Why had her father told her such a story? What kind of cruel intentions could be behind a lie that horrible? Armando pondered the question, realizing after a moment that he'd at least learned the answer to one mystery; Lauren obviously hadn't seen whoever had shot her mother. He searched his mind for his own memories of that night. He was certain he hadn't seen a gun in Margaret Stanley's hand. It'd been lying on the floor, not in her hand. He remembered because he'd wondered why it had been left. If a burglar had killed her, as had been reported, the last thing he would have done was leave behind a valuable weapon.

Which meant that someone had altered the murder scene after Armando had gone.

So for years, Lauren had believed her mother had committed suicide and she'd absorbed the deception as the gospel truth. She'd absorbed it so well, in fact, that she'd come to feel responsible for the death. The families of suicide victims, especially children who couldn't understand, often felt the same way, but the guilt in Lauren's voice had pricked him. She was doubly innocent, but she could never know.

If he told her the truth and eliminated her anxieties, she would realize he had been there.

If he told her nothing and maintained his silence, she would be forever haunted by her past.

Late that afternoon, his final patient limped into the examination room with a painful grimace. He was a farmer and he had a nasty wound on his left ankle, the result of a careless turn of his ax while clearing some land, he explained between groans.

As Armando gently lifted the man's foot and began to examine it, the door squeaked open. Lauren stepped into the room, then stopped when she saw the patient. "Oh! I'm sorry! I didn't know you were still busy—" She began to retreat.

"Don't go!" Armando called. "You can help me. Zue's gone to visit her sister and I need some assistance."

The expression on her face remained tentative. "I know CPR but that's the extent of my medical skills—"

Ignoring her disclaimer, Armando motioned her forward. "All I need is something from the drug case." He jerked his chin toward the locked cabinet behind him. "You can handle that, can't you? The keys are on my belt."

She came closer, her eyes averted from the man's foot. "I can do that," she said, "as long as no one's bleeding."

"Just get the key ring and don't look. I need the white bottle on the bottom shelf and one of the glass vials beside it. You'll have to unlock the smaller glass door that fronts the shelf. I keep the narcotics double locked."

Lauren did as he instructed. Replacing his keys a moment later, her fingers brushed his arm and he felt a spark from the contact. He'd become increasingly sensitive to her nearness and, much to his dismay, the vulnerability she'd shared with him last night had only served to heighten it.

He spoke to distract himself. "Don't tell me you're scared of a little blood."

She put the medicine on the table beside him. "I'm scared of everything," she said. "There isn't a phobia out there I haven't had the pleasure of meeting."

Armando looked at her over the farmer's foot. "You handle them quite well."

"I didn't know there was another choice."

"There are always other choices." He thought of the lie she'd been told. "But I wouldn't recommend most of them."

He finished cleaning and wrapping the

man's wound, then he gave him the pain-killers Lauren had retrieved, along with some instructions on how to take them. The poor farmer hobbled out, and Armando began to tidy up the room. Zue would clean everything more thoroughly later but he liked to leave things neat. He spoke to Lauren as he wiped down the cabinet. "So what brings you here?"

"I wanted to tell you about my phone call last night. When I spoke with my father I told him about the guide."

She'd come to Armando's office after dinner so she could phone Dallas. Armando had gone outside to give her some privacy but he'd wondered how J. Freeman Stanley had reacted to her explanation of Peña's fate.

Armando resumed his efforts, but paid no attention to what he was doing. "What did he say?"

"He said what he always does. He told me to come home," she answered. "But he almost sounded frightened. I was surprised."

"If you had a daughter and the same

thing had happened to her, you would want her home, too."

"Maybe," she said, "but there was more to his response than that. I don't think my father is someone who panics but that's exactly how I'd be tempted to describe his reaction to what I told him."

"Why do you think that was the case?"

"I don't know." She pursed her lips and leaned against the counter at her back, crossing her arms. "He definitely wants me to come back, though. As quickly as possible."

His thoughts going in a different direction, Armando responded by rote, the explanation pat. "Peru holds bad memories for him, considering your mother's death. It might not be rational, but perhaps he fears he might lose you here, as well."

She stared at him, her blue eyes thoughtful. "I never considered that possibility before."

He took off his white coat and hung it on the hook behind the door. "You aren't supposed to think that way," he said. "You're a writer, not a psychiatrist."

He took her elbow and directed her toward the hallway, turning out the light, then closing the door behind them. "Be grateful," he instructed with a smile. "Psychiatrists are very scary people."

FOR THE REST OF THE EVENING, Lauren thought about her father's pleas. So far, she'd resisted his appeals to come home, but perhaps it was time to reconsider. Armando had made it clear he wasn't going to help her; there was nothing else keeping her in Peru. Maybe she should go on to Machu Picchu, do her research and then head back to Dallas. She couldn't justify staying any longer, could she?

She woke up at 2:00 a.m. in a sweat, the echo of her scream dying in the empty hospital ward. After her fear subsided, anger settled in and she threw off the tangled blankets, grabbed Zue's robe and headed for the door. She was sick and tired of trying to battle her subconscious for sleep. If she couldn't get any rest, then she might as well get some fresh air. Maybe she'd come to a decision about leaving. Stepping outside, she was greeted by a landscape lit by a full moon. A spotlight couldn't have provided more illumination and she started for the path that circled the compound. She'd walked it so many times since she'd arrived, she would have known the way in a blizzard.

She rounded the corner that went past Armando's cabin, then halted abruptly. He was sitting outside, in a rocker beside his front door, the small glow of a lit cigar giving away his presence. The scent of the smoke reminded her of the cigars her father had occasionally indulged in when she'd been a child.

"It's all right," Armando said from the shadows. "I promise I won't attack you this time. You're safe."

Lauren walked toward him slowly. She wasn't as sure as he was of her well-being. Despite her disappointment over his refusal to help her, she continued to be drawn to him in a way she didn't understand. He wasn't like any of the men she knew back in Dallas; in fact, he wasn't like anyone she'd ever met before. There were secrets behind that black gaze that she knew he'd never share with anyone, least of all her, even though she suspected she knew some of them already.

"I don't want to intrude," she said as she neared. "I just couldn't sleep so I decided to take a walk."

"You aren't intruding on anything," he assured her. "In fact, if you don't mind, I might join you." He tamped out the cigar then placed it in a small crystal bowl on the table beside his chair.

"I don't mind at all," she replied, then her eyes went to the heavy glass, its etched surface glinting in the moon's silver light. "That's some ashtray you've got. It looks as if it belongs in a palace instead of out here in the jungle."

He came to where she was waiting and took her hand, tucking it into his elbow as they began to stroll. The chivalrous gesture seemed almost as incongruous as what she'd just pointed out.

"It *does* belong in a palace," he said, surprising her. "My great great great grandfather was a fallen member of the court of Spain during the late 1700s. It wasn't a good time to be a royal and he fled Europe when Spain made peace with France in 1795. The bowl came with him."

She stared at him open-mouthed. "And you use it?"

"It survived this long, a few more years won't hurt it."

"But something like that must be priceless."

"It's only a piece of glass."

"But it means something to you," she argued, "or you wouldn't have it with you."

When he swung his gaze to hers, she saw a spark of amusement. "You're a perceptive person."

"Not really," she said. "That's just common sense."

He shrugged. "Call it what you will, but you are right. It *does* mean something to me." He lifted his left arm and she saw a flash of gold. For some reason, she couldn't take her eyes from the heavy gold links around his wrist.

"My bracelet came from him, too. I keep them both to remind myself of what matters in this world. He abandoned his country and all he took with him was a piece of crystal and a few chunks of gold. When I die, I want to leave more than that for my grandchildren."

He dropped his arm and she lifted her eyes. Her curiosity piqued, she couldn't help herself. "Like what?"

"I'm not sure," he confessed. "But it won't be something material, even if that was what I wanted. Working here is not increasing my bottom line."

"If you had stayed with your practice, you would be a very rich man now. And a famous one, too."

"Having money isn't important. I've had it."

"So what does matter, then?"

He slowed to a stop and looked thoughtful. "Doing the right thing," he said. "And making the world a better place. That is what matters to me now."

She stared at him in surprise. "Those are terrific goals. There's nothing wrong with them."

"I agree." He resumed his walking and she fell into step with him. "But not everyone shares your opinion."

"Who could disagree with something like that?"

"You'd be surprised. One man's purpose is another man's wickedness."

His voice was teasing, but Lauren had heard this before. She fit the pieces into the puzzle and then stopped their progress by tightening her fingers against his arm.

"You really mean that, don't you? You're working here and giving your time to these people because you're trying to fix the universe." She studied his face in the filtered light. "You didn't come here to hide," she said slowly, "you came here to atone—for your sins and everyone else's...."

HER PROJECTION WAS OBVIOUS but Armando didn't argue with her.

"I'm not sure I'd agree with that. *Atone* is a strong term," he said. She stood in the moonlight and stared at him, her need for more explanation clear in her expression.

He waved toward a pair of lawn chairs at the edge of the clearing. "It's a long story. Shall we sit?"

"I think I may need to," she answered, "judging by the look on your face."

"Don't worry." He smiled in an effort to lessen the tension that had suddenly knotted inside him. They each took a chair. "My story will bore you beyond belief."

"Somehow I doubt that."

"I'm telling you the truth—because there's nothing different about it. Latin America is full of the haves and the have-nots. I came from the former—a very wealthy family. My father was—and still is—a very well-known psychiatrist in Buenos Aires. My mother is a psychologist. When I was growing up, I lacked for nothing. We had maids, cooks, gardeners.

A host of employees ran our homes and our lives. It was expected that I would follow in my parents' footsteps and I did just that. I *wanted* to become a psychiatrist. The way the mind worked was a fascinating thing to me."

"So you were born to the profession. Your reputation developed before you were even out of medical school."

"It came far before I was prepared. I had a long way to go in my studies but like all young medical students, I was eager to start saving the world. I volunteered in the free clinics on my days off and tried to hone my skills as fast as I could. I was fascinated by dreams and concentrated my therapy there. I had plenty of clients. My fellow students began to talk and before I knew what was happening, even they were coming to me for help with their dreams."

"You must have been flattered."

"I was terrified."

She arched an eyebrow. "Why?"

"The responsibility was too much. I didn't want to tell the future or read minds, which is what they thought I was doing. I'd gone to medical school to heal and these patients were looking for miracles."

"But you were helping them."

"Yes," he conceded. "I *was* helping them. But not in a way that made sense to me. At that point, I didn't understand the process. My life felt as it were out of control."

"What did your parents think about your gift?"

He flinched at the label she chose but he answered. "My mother was as mystified as I was, but my father was thrilled. He's more of a businessman than a doctor. He saw the possibilities and wanted to capitalize on my patients' faith in me."

"You could have done that very easily." She paused. "I did a lot of reading before I decided to seek you out, Armando. The interpretation of dreams is a very tricky subject. Some people put it right up there with palm reading and tarot cards but you had a flawless name. You were very well thought of in the community."

"I know," he answered regretfully. "But

people are right to be skeptical. I wasn't lying when I told you dreams do not foresee what's ahead or hold magical explanations. They make sense only within the context of the dreamer's life. You can't pull their relevance out of the air. I understood people and *that* is why I understood their dreams. There was no magic to it."

"I see what you're saying but I'm not sure I agree. Maybe that's how your father felt."

"My father didn't care," he said bluntly. "He knew Argentina and he knew how the people would react. It is a country with two faces, as I've said. He believed I could expand his practice with my talents, and he had more wealthy patients than he could handle. He wanted me to do parlor tricks for bored housewives who were anxious about their next adventure in plastic surgery. I wasn't interested. I wanted to help the people who couldn't afford his soft leather couch."

"And he wasn't happy with your choice."

Armando laughed dryly. "My father is a very controlling individual. I had already angered him with my politics and this only added fuel to the fire—for both of us. I rejected him and then I rejected my training. I treated broken legs and bullet wounds and anything else that I could as long as the ailment was physical and not mental. The more injustice I saw, the more rebellious I became. I put aside my psychiatric training at that point and I've never looked back."

CHAPTER SEVEN

LAUREN TOOK ONE LOOK at Armando's expression and instantly forgot her earlier uneasiness. Despite the careless way he'd described his past, he *was* atoning. He clearly felt he'd disappointed his father and let his whole family down.

She put her hand on his arm and moved closer. "You did what you thought was best. You can't fulfill another person's desires. You have to live your life the way you see fit."

"I'm well aware of that now." He covered her fingers with his then he stood and pulled her to her feet. "I was young and foolish back then, though. And in the culture of my family, you did what Father expected."

"That's a universal theme," Lauren said,

distracted by his touch. "We all want to please our parents."

He considered her pronouncement, then spoke softly. "You say that as if you failed at it yourself. I can't imagine any father being displeased with a daughter like you."

"I wasn't an easy child," she explained. "Especially after my mother died. I had problems with her death."

"Who wouldn't?"

Lauren looked off into the light-swallowing jungle. "Someone more stable, I suppose. I didn't handle the whole affair too well."

"Anyone would be traumatized by a loss that important. The circumstances—and your age—made it even worse."

The sympathy in his voice reverberated inside her. She'd never known a man so warm and kindhearted but, at the same time, so tough, as well.

"I spent a lot of time in analysis afterward. With Dr. Gladney," she mused. "I can see now how surprised my father was when I didn't even remember *her!*"

"Did your therapy help?"

"No." Her answer was blunt but genuine. "Nothing helped but time. And now, I'm not so sure about that. I feel like I've taken a step backward by coming here when all I meant to do was try to go forward."

His hands slid up her arms, his eyes filling with an emotion she sensed he was fighting against. "You're still a young woman, Lauren. You have a lot of years left to work this out. Perhaps you should be more patient with yourself on this issue."

"I don't need patience." She spoke as plainly as she knew how. "I need clarity."

He frowned with uncertainty and before she could stop herself, Lauren lifted her hands to his jaw. Under her fingers, his beard was rough. It provided a sharp contrast to the empathy in his manner.

"I need clarity," she repeated, "and I won't get it until I understand what happened that night. And I mean what *really* happened."

Sometime during the conversation, his hands had gone to her waist and, as she spoke, he took another step closer. Their faces, bathed with moonlight, were inches apart. When he spoke, his breath touched her cheek. "The truth will come when it's time and not before. That's how it always works."

He looked into her eyes and then directly into her heart. Or at least, that's how it felt at the time, she thought later. At that moment, though, her mind went blank and all she could think to say was "I don't want to wait."

"Neither do I," he answered softly. Then he pulled her into his arms and began to kiss her.

HE'D MEANT TO DISTRACT HER but at the touch of Lauren's lips, *he* became the one to lose track of what was happening.

Her soft curves and natural perfume filled his senses, her body an attraction he couldn't resist. He nudged her mouth open with his tongue as the temptation turned into something more than he'd planned.

Much, much more.

Her hands snaked around his neck and then she threaded her fingers through his hair, her touch tentative yet somehow all the more sensual because of it. A low moan built in the back of her throat and the sound resonated inside Armando, an echo of the desire he could feel swelling inside himself.

For a second longer than he should have, Armando toyed with letting their actions continue, but only for a second. The possibilities—and their resulting entanglements—were too disastrous even to consider.

He retreated reluctantly, his gaze meeting Lauren's somewhat dazed one. "I'm sorry. This is not what you came here for. I shouldn't have—"

She quickly recovered her composure, a polished look slipping over her features. He imagined the mask was something she wore a lot back home. "Don't say we shouldn't have kissed. I hate it when someone says that."

He found himself smiling. "I can't imagine you hear *that* too frequently."

She returned his smile, but her expression was false. "I guess I don't, but when a moment like that happens, it just happens. Let's leave things like that." She glanced upward before letting her eyes come back to his. "We can blame it on the moonlight."

"Maybe you can do that," he said. "But I can't. I've been thinking about kissing you for quite some time."

He spoke the truth. Something about Lauren Stanley was tunneling under the wall he'd built a long time before to protect himself.

"I'm flattered," she said. "You haven't exactly seen me at my best."

She was right but not in the way she thought. He took her cue and joked. "Your worst days would be anyone else's best ones."

The compliment did what he expected it would. She chuckled, shook her head and took a step back, their embrace now broken. "You truly are the quintessential Latin, Armando. You know exactly what to say, don't you?"

"You give me more credit than I deserve," he answered.

Her mask slipped for a second. "I doubt that," she said quietly. "I doubt that very seriously."

DISTURBED BY THE DESIRE Armando's kiss had fueled, Lauren was quiet as he led her back to the hospital ward.

She didn't understand how she could be so attracted to him when he'd made it clear he wasn't going to help her.

Even more to the point, she didn't understand how she could be so attracted to him when she thought he might be a killer.

He opened the door for her then paused. "Try to get some sleep," he advised. "You still need the rest."

"I'll have time for that when I get back to Dallas."

He stared at her. "Have you decided to return?"

"There's no reason for me to stay here any longer," she said. "Is there?"

He didn't answer and his eyes remained unreadable.

She smiled despite her disappointment. "I didn't think so."

Turning, she took a step inside but she stopped when he spoke.

"You're a strong woman, Lauren. You'll find what you need inside yourself."

"I hope so."

His voice went soft. "I know so."

He was gone a moment later, and for a long time, Lauren stared at the spot where he'd been before she went inside, her decision made. His arms had felt too good, his caress too warm.

It was time to give up and go home before she did something she would come to regret.

Her decision to leave, as hard as it was to make, seemed to free something inside her. She went back to bed and immediately fell asleep, her nightmares, for once, leaving her alone.

The memory of Armando's kiss hit her as soon as she awoke the following morning. She didn't want to think about it so she switched her thoughts to the plans she had to make. Getting out of the bed, she saw a breakfast tray on her nightstand. With Zue gone, there was only one person who would have brought it to her—Armando. Her heart pounded at the idea of him standing beside her bed, but she forced herself to think about everything she needed to do. Travel arrangements back to Cuzco. New supplies. New guide. Airline tickets to Dallas. The list seemed endless but, suddenly, it didn't matter.

A burning sensation started in her throat and then spread into her chest. Lauren gasped as the pain registered, the china slipping from her fingers to crash to the floor and shatter.

She followed it down a moment later.

MONDAYS WERE RESERVED for children. They came in with sore throats and skinned knees and upset tummies. With Zue still gone and no help in sight, he prepared for a busy day. Armando didn't hear his name being called until the yard man burst inside the examining room and interrupted him.

"*¡Doctor! ¡Doctor!* Come quick! *¡Venga rápidamente! ¡Apresúrese!*"

Armando started to chastise the man, then he caught the look of panic on his face. "What it is?" he asked with alarm.

"*¡La señorita!*"

Thrusting the girl he'd been about to examine back into her mother's arms, Armando tore out of the room to follow the gardener back to the ward, his mind flooding with terrible possibilities.

He'd spotted Lauren through the open window, the yard man said. She looked dead.

At first glance, Armando agreed. Unconscious and unmoving, she was stretched out on the floor still wearing her pajamas. Shards of a broken teacup were scattered about and, a foot from her outstretched fingers, a pill bottle lay on the floor.

He picked up the empty container and read the label, cursing loudly before he turned back to her. Her pupils were tiny, her pulse slow. Her breathing was shallow but she moaned as he turned her head to the side, and he let out a sigh of relief. She *wasn't* dead.

At least not yet.

THE FIRST THING Lauren saw when she opened her eyes was Armando. He was asleep beside her bed in a chair, his legs stretched out before him at an awkward angle, his head resting against the back of the wooden frame. He looked uncomfortable and exhausted. She moved, then caught her breath sharply, a foreign ache rippling through her body.

He jumped to his feet, coming to her side before she could even speak. "You're awake," he said. *"¡Dé gracias a Dios!"* Taking her wrist, he proceeded to check her pulse.

"What happened?" she asked. "I feel like I got run over by a train."

He released her, but his eyes stayed on her face. "You don't remember?"

She shook her head then winced. "We went for a walk," she said. "I came back. I went to bed." She frowned in confusion and stopped to think. "When I got up, I had a cup of tea," she said. "Then that was it."

"We found you on the floor." He retrieved a small plastic bottle from his pocket and handed it to her. "This was beside you."

She read the label. "I don't recognize the name. What is it?"

He took the container back. "This held a very powerful painkiller," he replied. "I gave some of it to the farmer who came in on Saturday with the ax wound. You got it out of the cabinet for me."

"I did?"

"You don't remember that, either?"

"No. I recall getting the medicine for you because I had to get your keys out—but I didn't look at the label and even if I had, I wouldn't have known what the drug was."

Armando stared at her and said nothing, and it took her a second to make the connection. She would have laughed except for the expression on his face. She sat up and gripped the sheets. "Armando! Please don't tell me you think I somehow took those keys and—"

"I wasn't trying to—"

She interrupted him again. "Who brought me that tea?"

"One of the girls from the kitchen. I already talked to her. She brought me some from the very same pot."

"Well, there was something different in mine. There had to be."

"She said—"

"I don't care what she said," Lauren interrupted him. "Test my blood."

"I already have. The sample's been sent to Cuzco."

"Good," she said. "Because I'm telling you the truth. I didn't take those pills. Why on earth would I do something like that? Think about it."

"If you'd let me speak, I would have said that is exactly what I do *not* want to do." He put his fists on the edge of the bed. "Unfortunately, however, I *have* thought about it and I can't ignore my conclusion. Someone must have come in here and put something in your tea. They left the bottle to make it look like suicide."

Her astonishment turned into horror and she felt her eyes go wide. "Oh, my God… What's going on, Armando? Why on earth would someone want me dead? First the bridge, now this…." Her questions came out in a tumble of confusion. "Who's behind this? And why? Do you think they followed me down here from the States? I don't know a soul here."

He shrugged. "Peru is not the safest of countries. It could be very easy to label any disaster an accident. To make a murder look like suicide."

Armando's answer made sense but the way he delivered the pronouncement—so coolly, so confidently—sent a shiver skipping down Lauren's spine. Death was a casual subject to him and she was afraid she knew why.

She knew he was telling the truth, but she remained incredulous. "I guess that's believable, but it still doesn't answer the who part. It's not like I'm important or anything." She shook her head again. "That doesn't make any kind of sense."

"Murder rarely does."

She swallowed. "Where do we go from here?"

"I've been thinking about that, too," he said. "And I've decided the answer is Rojo. We need to visit with Joaquin Peña's brother."

CHAPTER EIGHT

ZUE AND BELI CAME BACK Tuesday afternoon. Horrified to learn of Lauren's "accident" with the tea, Zue was mystified by who could have done such a thing. The old woman had been with him for years, so Armando wouldn't have doubted her even if she'd been around, but he felt differently about Beli. The night before Lauren's accident, he'd seen a light on in Zue's cabin. At the time, he'd thought nothing of it, but later Armando had wondered. Beli and Joaquin Peña had been friends. Maybe the older boy had convinced Zue's grandson to poison Lauren? But why? And when? And for that matter, why would Joaquin have cut the bridge while she was crossing it?

Armando had no answers to those questions, but he knew one thing—if for some reason Beli had remained behind when Zue had left, he could have easily slipped something into Lauren's tea.

Armando had questioned the boy without mercy but while he'd been shaken by Armando's queries, Beli had stuck to his story, his eyes dilated and wild. He'd been with his grandmother the whole time, he'd insisted, and she would back him up. When Armando had asked Zue about it, she'd done exactly as Beli had said.

Sitting in his office that evening, Armando knew it was impossible to make sense of what was happening without considering what had transpired in the past. There had to be a connection between Margaret Stanley's murder and the attempts on Lauren's life, but even if he uncovered it, what could he do about the situation?

The answer was simple; he could do nothing.

He was powerless and he couldn't stop what was happening any more than he could stop the attraction that was growing between him and Lauren. To fight the inevitable seemed pointless but he had to try because he had no other choice. Not really.

He nodded to himself. If she left, the battle would end, but she wasn't leaving now. He would have made the same decision himself, but he would never tell her that. For as long as he drew breath, he'd continue to try and make her return to Dallas. He'd have to be obscure about his goal, though. Lauren was too smart to be easily manipulated.

Armando was sinking, slowly but surely, into a bottomless quagmire. He walked outside, the cries of the night birds filling the air, the eerie sounds somehow soothing. He hoped he was doing the right thing by taking her to Rojo.

If he wasn't, they were both heading for some very big trouble.

LAUREN CALLED HER FATHER that evening as promised, but it wasn't a conversation she enjoyed. And there was no way she was going to tell him Armando thought someone might be after her. Her father would be on the next plane down to physically drag her back to Dallas.

"When are you coming home?" He started the call with the same question each time.

"I don't know yet," she answered, as she always did, then added, "Things have gotten a little complicated here."

"Complicated? What does that mean?"

She made the explanation as simple as possible. "I drank some…bad tea. It set me back a bit."

"Are you all right? What kind of tea was this?" His voice rose in alarm. "What were your symptoms—"

"It was nothing. I'm fine now," she said firmly. "Dr. Torres took excellent care of me, as he has all along."

And *that* certainly wasn't a lie, she thought. Armando had saved her life twice now. In a karmic sense, she was pretty sure that meant she owed him even more. Whatever the debt was, paying it would be easy. Armando's generous nature made her want to follow his lead and give back to him in return.

"Where did this tea come from, Lauren? Did anyone else drink it?"

She focused again on her father. "The kitchen at the hospital prepared the tea," she said.

"Was it food poisoning?"

"Dr. Torres did some blood work. The results aren't in yet—it may take a while."

"Come back to Dallas, Lauren. Dr. Gladney is anxious to see you."

"I'm sure she is," Lauren said. "But I'm not ready to return just yet. There are things I have to do here, Dad."

"Like what?"

"I want to finish my article. You always taught me not to leave work undone."

"I think this warrants an exception." He sounded more uptight than usual. "Your health is at stake. Your mental *and* physical health. I should never have listened to Cunningham."

The attaché's face came instantly into her mind and she found herself surprised.

It was strange how quickly the blanks in her memory had been filled. "You spoke with Daniel?"

"I called him before you even left," her father confessed. "I didn't mention it because I didn't want to upset you in case you didn't remember him, but I wanted his reassurance that the political situation in that part of the world was safe. He's still with the State Department and stationed in Pakistan. I thought he'd have more up-to-date information than I had access to. He told me things were fine and said you'd be perfectly all right. After you went missing I phoned him again but he was out of the country at that point."

"That's when you called Armando's friend?"

"Yes."

"Well, it's a good thing you didn't talk to him directly. It'd be embarrassing. I'm all right, Dad," she reassured him. "I need to do this. I need to spend some time here."

"Why?" The question held more anguish than she'd heard from him during all their previous discussions. "You can't make things happen any differently, Lauren. The past is over. Let it go and come home."

"I can't." She didn't want her father to think she didn't appreciate what he'd done in dealing with her and her difficult childhood but she had to be honest. "I suspect you know why, too." She paused. "I came here specifically to see Dr. Torres. You had to have known that all along."

A tense silence built up over the phone line. "I don't think the man can help you. He's a charlatan, Lauren, and any well-respected doctor would side with me on that."

"If you feel that way, why did you have journals about his work in your office? I saw them so don't deny it."

"I take dozens of different professional journals, Lauren. Some of them don't always vet their articles—or authors—as they should. The fact that you saw something in my library doesn't mean I follow the man's philosophy."

"What would you say if I told you that he'd refused to help me?"

"I'd say thank God, then tell you to come home."

She closed her eyes. "I can't do that, Dad. I'm sorry…but I just can't do that. Not until I find the truth."

"And what will you do when you find it?"

His question surprised her. "I don't know," she answered. "But I have to keep looking until then."

THEY HEADED FOR ROJO on Friday, Armando gunning the bike over the trail, despite the ruts. Lauren seemed to have recovered from her ordeal with no lingering ill effects, her mood quieter and more pensive than usual. Armando was curious, as always, about her phone call to her father, but he stayed silent, as well. They reached the tiny village before noon and Armando was glad the trip was over. Having her pressed against his body for that long hadn't been comfortable.

He parked, pulled off his helmet, then swung a leg over the bike, a tiny cloud of dust and grime puffing up from beneath his boots. "Joaquin's brother lives down this street and over one. We'll leave the bike and walk to his house."

She nodded and undid the strap of her own helmet, her hair tumbling over her shoulders like a waterfall. "Is it safe for your motorcycle here?"

"Probably not," he answered ruefully, "but there'll be more witnesses if someone does steal it."

They crossed the street, two chickens and a rooster scattering with a squawk as they reached the curb, the tumble of trash the birds had been pecking at set free by a sudden gust of wind. Expecting to see disgust on her face, Armando took a quick look at Lauren. Her expression registered nothing but determination, the layers of poverty and dirt going unnoticed.

They reached the Peña residence after five minutes of walking, Ben Williamson's description more apt than Armando had expected. A small fenced area to the left of the shack contained three underfed goats. On the right side, there were four pigs.

Two dogs, each scratching their hindquarters, sat on the front porch and stared with apathetic eyes. At their approach, one gave a halfhearted bark, then fell silent. Having lived in South America all his life, Armando was generally unmoved by such things, but the poverty rising from this home seemed ingrained. Nothing was going to change it.

He was still surveying the area when the gate squeaked. He turned in time to see that Lauren had pulled back the latch and was already going up the sidewalk. He followed. Apparently alerted by the same sound as Armando, someone emerged from the front door to stand on the porch.

Dirty and unshaven, the man behind the rickety railing was probably closer to thirty than he was twenty but his face belonged to someone in his fifties. His jaw bulged with a wad of something and he spit over the railing of the porch as Armando addressed him. "Are you the brother of Joaquin Peña?"

"*Sí.*" His voice was low and guttural, a

surly belligerence behind it. "I am Arturo Peña. What do you want?"

"Ben Williamson told me about your brother," Armando said politely. "I was very sorry to hear about your loss."

"He should have known better," the man pronounced.

"Known what?" Armando asked.

"He got mixed up with a bad crowd," Peña answered. "If he owed you money, you can forget—"

Armando held out his palms. "No, no. We're not here for that."

"Then what?"

Lauren came from behind Armando. "I met your brother at the train station several weeks ago. He offered to guide me to the ruins."

Arturo Peña's face twisted in confusion. "What are you talking about? My brother was no guide."

"I figured that out. He left me before we reached the ruins—"

"No money." He started backing up,

shaking his head with more force than before. "I'm not giving you anything—"

"I don't want money," she said hastily. "This isn't about money."

He stopped. "Then what?"

"We want to know if he said anything to you about the nearest bridge between Cuzco and Qunico," Armando interjected. "Did he mention it was damaged?"

Reaching into a small woven sack at his waist, Peña pulled out a handful of dried leaves that resembled tobacco. He stuffed them into his jaw, his eyes never leaving their faces. "Damaged how?" he said from around the lump.

"That's what we'd like to know," Armando answered. "The bridge broke when the *señorita* tried to cross. She fell into the river. Did Joaquin talk to you about the incident?"

Arturo's fingers worked the pouch on his belt as he considered the question. Glancing toward the side yard, Armando spotted the man's garden. In contrast to the rest of the place, it was well-cared for, sporting tomato plants and a tall, healthy bush with thin oval leaves. The flowers were small and clustered and some of the lower branches had been stripped of leaves, just as Armando had expected they would be. To the left of the tomatoes, another smaller, shorter bush sat closer to the shack. It was partially hidden but Armando recognized its long, slender leaves, too.

Peña spoke up, his voice abrupt. "I don't know anything about it." He started to go back inside when the sound of a slamming door broke the silence. The little porch seemed to shimmy from the force as Peña cursed loudly and a figure shot from the backyard past the three of them to the street out front. Armando caught a fleeting impression of a faded black Metallica T-shirt and a running teenager but he needed nothing more.

Armando turned back to the man. "Did you have company? We didn't mean to interrupt."

Arturo Peña raised a palsied hand and

swatted it though the air. *"Nada, nada,"* he said. "It's nothing. And I have nothing for you, either." With another hostile glance at Lauren, he shuffled inside the house.

ARMANDO LED LAUREN OFF the porch and back to the street. "I don't know about you," he said when they reached the sidewalk, "but I feel the need for some coffee." He looked down at his watch, then back at her. "It's almost lunchtime. Think you could handle it?"

Disappointed by how little they'd learned, Lauren nodded but said nothing. They walked toward the square, Armando directing them to what he said was the only *restaurante* in town. "I've eaten here several times," he said as he pulled the door open for her, "and I survived."

"That's some recommendation."

He laughed. "The *rocote relleno* is actually pretty good."

Lauren started to reply but stopped, the stares that followed them as they entered too pointed to ignore. "What's wrong?"

she whispered as they headed to the back and found an empty table.

"Rojo doesn't get too many visitors," Armando said quietly. "Forget about it. They still stare at me sometimes and I'm not even blond."

Lauren smiled uncertainly at him. The waitress handed them menus, took their drink orders, then disappeared into the kitchen.

Armando put the plastic card down after a quick look. "Like I said, I'd recommend the stuffed peppers," he advised. "But whatever you do, don't order the *cuy*."

She cringed. "I was horrified when my father explained what it really was."

"Someone once told me they found *cuy* bones at Machu Picchu."

"That's interesting…but it's still not a delicacy I'd suggest the average tourist try."

"Guinea pig has been eaten in this part of the world for years." Armando shrugged. "It's a tradition—no different than Arturo's *chacchar*."

Lauren frowned. "His what?"

"His chew. Didn't you see him spitting?"

She felt a ripple of revulsion. "I tried not to notice."

"The pouch he wore at his waist is called a *chuspa*. Sometimes they call it a *huallqui*. It holds a little bit of *uipta*—"

"Ashes?" she translated in a puzzled voice. "Ashes of what?"

"From the quinoa plant. Sometimes they carry pulverized lime, too."

"Why?"

"They use it to mix with the other item in the bag. It makes it taste better."

"And that would be…?"

"His day's supply of coca leaves."

"Coca, as in 'cocaine'?"

"The indigenous people chew it," he explained. "And they have for centuries, especially around here. He had a coca bush in the yard. The harvest just finished so he probably has a nice fresh crop. The leaves are picked in March, when the rains stop, then again in June and November."

"That can't be too good for you."

Armando reached for the bottle of water

that was on their table and filled their glasses. "It's the culture," he answered. "The priests had to chew it or their sacrifices weren't accepted by the gods. The miners think it softens the ore if you spit on the veins." He sipped his water. "It's common around here."

"Well, it didn't seem to loosen his lips any, did it?" Lauren wrapped her fingers around her water glass and stared over the table, her earlier discontent returning. "I was hoping he'd tell us more."

"Did you really expect that?"

"Maybe I didn't expect it," she confessed, "but I was hoping for it."

"I wasn't. But that doesn't mean we didn't learn anything."

She jerked her eyes to his face. "What do you mean?"

"He had an interesting bush in his yard," Armando said carefully. "It's called *la planta durmiente.*"

"The sleeping plant?"

"That's right," he said. "Its leaves can be used as a sedative."

"That's good."

"They put it in tea."

She stilled.

"An overdose can kill you."

Lauren felt the blood leave her face and she blinked, her hand going to her throat. "Do you think that's what I drank?"

"I don't know," he answered. "That's quite a coincidence, don't you think?"

"Not really."

He nodded his understanding. "Did you get a good look at the kid who ran by?"

"I was so surprised to see someone that I wasn't prepared. I did wonder why he left so abruptly, though."

"He heard Arturo's footsteps," Armando said with confidence. "He thought we were all going inside. He didn't want to be seen."

Once again, Lauren felt a chill come over at his analysis of the situation. Armando functioned in two very different worlds—the one of healing and another one she didn't want to name.

"Did you see who he was?" she asked.

"I caught some writing on the T-shirt,

but that's about it. It had a band's name across the front. I didn't recognize him."

She knew instantly that Armando was lying but, before she could ask, their food arrived. By the time the waitress finished putting everything on the table, the moment was lost. Armando's expression closed once more, and Lauren knew she'd get nothing else from him.

ARMANDO PUSHED BACK from the table and let his eyes wander over the other diners. The patrons were locals for the most part, but one of the area's ever-present hikers was hunched over a bowl of *chupe de pollo* in the corner. He wasn't facing them, but his shaggy hair and disheveled clothing, not to mention his huge black backpack, made him easy to spot. Throngs of tourists passed through as they walked the Inca Trail, some old, some young, some rich, some poor.

Armando watched Lauren pick at her food. She'd eaten very little, their meeting with Joaquin Peña's brother obviously still on her mind. Armando de-cided it best to pull her attention in another direction, at least until he could investigate more.

The waitress came and they asked for coffee as she took their plates. He leaned his elbows on the table. "Tell me about the magazine that you write for. Do you give rich tourists advice on where to eat and what to buy when they get to their luxury resort? So they don't, God forbid, encounter something indigenous?"

She cocked her head and looked at him. "Not that you have any preconceived ideas on the subject, right?"

"I can talk about rich people like that," he said. "I used to be one."

"You don't strike me as someone who would be afraid to try a little *cuy*."

"I've lived in too many places and traveled too far to have a delicate stomach, or for that matter, a delicate anything. I just try to blend in and do my work."

She looked at him with a speculative gaze. "You *have* lived a varied life, it seems, but you've been in Peru for a long time, Armando. What happened to you in the time between your practice in Buenos Aires and your clinic in the jungle?"

This definitely wasn't the direction he'd wanted her to take. "I did just what I said I did. I traveled, lived in different places. Wandered from here to there."

"You aren't the kind of man who just wanders." Her gaze was steady.

"You don't know that," he answered. "Maybe I am."

She shook her head. "You're…what? Forty? Thirty-nine? You disappeared a few years after you finished med school. That's quite a gap."

The waitress brought their coffee and he sipped from his steaming mug to give himself some time to form an answer. "You've done your research."

"As much as I could."

She waited but Armando stayed quiet.

"If you don't tell me," she warned, "I'll make something up. I *am* a writer, you know."

He smiled. "Go ahead. Whatever you

concoct would be much more exciting than the truth. You've heard the whole tedious story of my past. Now I'm just a simple doctor and that's all I've ever been."

"A simple doctor? I don't think so…."

"You've had a much more glamorous life than I," he said. "Surely it was thrilling for you to leave the States as a child and come to a foreign country to live."

Adding sugar to her *café,* Lauren shook her head. "I hated it," she confessed. "The only bright spot in my world was my mother's attaché, a guy by the name of Daniel Cunningham. I had an enormous crush on him."

Daniel Cunningham had said nothing during their short friendship about the lonely young girl who'd been infatuated with him. But then, why would he? "He must have been flattered."

"I'm not sure he knew, although I can't see how he couldn't have. I was just a kid, but he was kind to me. My father actually contacted his office when he began to look for me because he's still with the State Department."

"Your father was very worried about you coming here."

"Peru's never been one of his favorite places. Neither one of us had wanted to move here but I didn't have a huge say in the matter and apparently, he didn't, either. Mom wanted us to come with her, so we came."

"Your father had a practice, I presume?"

"He did, and he also taught at a local psychiatric hospital. He worked with children, which was lucky for me, I guess."

"He helped you after your mother passed?"

"He did more than help. He kept me alive. Without him I would have been a goner."

"He probably feels the same way about you."

She stared at him with puzzled eyes. "What do you mean?"

"You gave him something to live *for*. He'd just lost his wife, surely he was as upset as you were."

She paused, mug in midair. "As bad as it

sounds, I never actually thought about it like that." She put down the coffee and dabbed her mouth with her napkin, her gaze going unfocused. "I was pretty out of it, but I never remember seeing him cry or being upset. He seemed almost unaffected by her death, but that couldn't possibly be the case. They'd been married for almost twenty years. Surely he must have loved her...."

He hid his disquiet. "We men are very good at hiding our true emotions," he suggested. "Perhaps he felt it would disturb you more if you witnessed his sadness."

Her eyes locked on his. "Would you be able to do that if you lost a wife you loved?"

Her question startled him so much he answered without thinking. "No. I could not disguise a grief that encompassing."

"I wouldn't be able to, either."

Armando looked away first, her frankness—and his—leaving him even more uncomfortable. He lightened the conversation after that, then they finished and he paid the bill as she walked outside. Waiting for his change, he turned to look at her through the plate-glass window. Lauren Stanley was far different from the person he'd expected her to be and, each time he thought he had her figured out, she seemed to surprise him. She was tougher, smarter and much more empathetic that he'd ever expected someone from her background to be.

He wasn't sure if that said more about her or more about him, but neither really mattered. They still didn't have a clue as to what was going on. Putting aside the question, he joined her outside the *restaurante* and they headed for his cycle.

CHAPTER NINE

THEY MADE GOOD TIME but the sun had already started to set when they pulled into the compound and headed for the shed where Armando kept the bike. He drove directly through the open double doors, parked and cut the engine. A silence that felt endless enveloped them.

Lauren was tired. And confused. And disappointed. She wondered how it would feel to lay her head on Armando's shoulders and simply rest for a bit. She knew she couldn't; she had some decisions to make and doing something like that wouldn't help her.

As if he shared her dilemma, Armando sat where he was for another moment, his legs still straddling the bike, his hands on his thighs. Finally, he stood and pulled off his helmet.

His hair was rumpled, his beard casting a heavy shadow on his jaw. "How do you feel?" he asked.

His eyes hid secrets, but there was sympathy in their depths and kindness, as well.

"Frustrated," she answered. "I was hoping we could find out more."

"I meant physically." He smiled. "How's your stomach?"

"Oh, that—I'm fine." With a look of chagrin, she swung her leg over the motorcycle's seat and stood, hanging her helmet by its strap off the handles. "I just wish I knew what to do next."

"You know what to do," he said softly. "You should go home. And get on with your life. You aren't going to find any answers here, Lauren."

"Even if someone's trying to kill me?"

"Maybe they aren't," he said. "I could be wrong, you know."

"And if you're not?"

"Then you'd be better protected in Dallas." He cradled her face with one of his hands, cutting off her protest. "You're too young and too beautiful to waste time doing this. Look forward. Forget about the past."

"It won't let me forget."

"*You* won't let yourself forget." He corrected her, his hand slipping to the back of her neck. His touch was hot, she realized, and his fingers felt rough. "*You* are in charge of this situation. No one else."

"You told me that before," she said. "But that's not how it feels."

They were standing in near darkness and his black eyes blended with the shadows. Still, she caught a gleam in them that made her shiver.

"You're chasing ghosts." It felt as if he tightened his grip but the change was so minute, she couldn't tell for sure. "And ghosts don't like to be caught."

"That's not true," she protested. "I came down here to chase *you*."

"My point exactly," he said. "I am no longer the doctor you're looking for and

I haven't been for years. Why don't you just go home and forget about this? I can't help you and I think you'd be much safer there, too."

This time when his fingers tightened, there was no mistaking it. She didn't know if she should feel comforted or afraid.

"You've had two very unfortunate accidents, Lauren. You almost drowned and you were poisoned. Either you're an awfully unlucky person or someone around here wants you gone. If I were you, I'd give that a lot of thought. Everyone's luck runs out eventually."

SHE STARED AT HIM with a questioning look, but instead of explaining further, Armando felt himself falling into the twin pools of Lauren's eyes.

She tensed beneath his touch, but she didn't move. His arms went around her and he pulled her closer, then a moment later, his lips captured hers.

She kissed him back and a mixture of emotions hit him that he could barely define, much less deal with in a reasonable manner. She was needy. She was courageous. She was sad. She was smart.

Her breasts pushed against his chest as his hands went down her spine to the curve of her hips and then lower. Beneath the full cotton skirt, he could feel her buttocks, smooth and firm. They fit into his palms perfectly. A groan started deep inside him and made its way out as his tongue parted her lips. When his hand came up and cradled one of her breasts, she moaned, as well.

Her desire seemed to match his own, Armando thought in surprise, and the realization made him want her even more. They were both adults, he told himself, pressing his body into hers, they had no other entanglements, they had no other lovers. What was the problem?

A voice inside his mind answered him even as he eased his hand beneath her sweater to feel her satin skin. *Ghosts don't like to be caught,* it said, mocking his advice to her only a minute earlier. *What will you do when all of yours are exposed?*

He caressed her breast, the lace of her bra the only thing between his flesh and hers. The barrier was thin and fragile but it was still an impediment and Armando's fingers pulled the fabric aside. He was rewarded instantly, the feel of her skin so sweet it made him moan again. Her nipple hardened as the sound of his desire echoed in the empty barn and he rubbed his thumb over the sensitive point. Unable to stop, but knowing he should, Armando felt he existed in a haze, his better judgment disappearing in the face of his overwhelming hunger for her.

Without any warning, someone spoke behind them.

LAUREN CAUGHT ONLY A GLIMPSE of a slim, short figure silhouetted inside the door frame of the shed. Before she could see more, Armando had spun around and thrust her behind him. The act of protection was too fast and too automatic. It felt like something a person who was accustomed to dangerous situations would do, not something a doctor would think of.

"Who's there?" he said sharply.

When the figure answered, Lauren realized it was Zue, and her voice sounded high and strained.

Armando replied to her query in impatient Quechuan and then she was gone. He turned back to Lauren. She couldn't see his expression but she didn't need to. His tone gave away his chagrin. "I have to go. Zue's niece is here. Her pregnancy hasn't been going well and things seem to be looking worse."

She'd understood *niece* and *worse* but nothing more. Almost grateful for the interruption, Lauren pushed slightly on his chest. They'd been reaching the point of no return.

"Go on," she said. "I can find my way back to my room."

He captured her hands with his and held them against his leather jacket. She thought she could feel his heart beating. "I will. But first I want to make sure you understand our conversation isn't over."

She tried to make fun of his threat. "This was a conversation?"

His gaze glimmered. "You know what I mean, Lauren. I believe you should seriously consider going home. You're in harm's way as long as you stay here."

"Don't you think I need to figure out why—"

"You can't figure out anything if you're dead."

His bluntness shocked her, just as he'd clearly planned. "I'll think about it," she said finally.

"That's fine," he said. "But don't think about it too long or the decision might be made for you."

He was still holding her, and she thought he was going to kiss her again, but he turned and left instead. Leaning against the bike, she let out a shaky sigh as he walked away.

ARMANDO MADE HIS WAY to the front of the compound, his attention going in three different directions. The kiss he'd just shared with Lauren was the stuff of fantasies. He was nuts to have taken her into his arms but what was even worse was the fact that he couldn't wait to do it again. The psycho-babble for which his profession was famous had several labels he could have used to describe his behavior but crazy worked as well as any of them.

He thrust aside his desire for Lauren and thought about Zue's niece but, a moment later, he put *her* problem aside and thought about Zue. He was ninety-nine percent sure the kid who'd shot out of Arturo Peña's house had worn a Metallica T-shirt. Faded and torn, the black shirt had caught Armando's eye because he knew of only one teenager in the area who owned a shirt like that—Beli, Zue's grandson. A hiker passing through had given it to the boy several years before and even though it was ragged and too small for him now, Beli persisted in wearing it at least once a week.

Normally, Armando wouldn't have given the boy's presence too much thought. Despite his grandmother's pleas, he'd hung out with Joaquin and his questionable friends for years, but after seeing the *planta durmiente* in Peña's front yard, Armando found himself having second… and third…thoughts.

Reaching the door of the clinic, Armando stepped inside and headed to the nearest examining room where he stripped off his jacket and shirt and began washing his hands and arms. He continued until his skin was red, then yanked a clean scrub over his head. He'd call Meredith as soon as he finished here and bring her up to date on the latest developments. The last time they'd talked, he'd been too rushed to do more than tell her about Lauren's belief her mother had killed herself. They'd discussed the situation briefly but Meredith had been as baffled as he was over the lie. Maybe she could help.

Zue was at his patient's side trying to calm her when he walked into the room. Putting all his other worries aside, Armando concentrated on the young woman stretched out on the table. She was carrying twins and high blood pressure had been plaguing her from the very beginning. Had she been a suburban housewife anywhere in the United States, he would have hospitalized her long before this, but she had four other children, all under five, and a working farm to care for, as well. When he'd told her to stay off her feet, she'd looked at him blankly.

He needed less time to get her stabilized than Zue had made him think he would. She was doing pretty well, all things considered, and he realized Zue was actually more nervous than the expectant mother. Turning to the older woman, he gave her instructions to call him if anything changed, otherwise, he said, he'd be back shortly. His nurse accepted his directions with a silent nod. If she'd seen what he and Lauren had been doing, she kept it to herself.

He started to leave but he paused when he reached the doorway. She looked up when he spoke.

"I was just wondering…" He tilted his head toward the other side of the compound. "Beli was supposed to finish the fence by the garden. Did he stay and get that job completed today?"

Her eyes were like two flat rocks and they gave away nothing. "The fence is done. I made sure of it."

She hadn't answered his question but Armando didn't press the matter. To do so would only bring attention to the issue and that was the last thing he wanted. "Good," he said. "I'm glad it's finished."

She returned to her niece without bothering to reply.

Back in his office, Armando called Meredith. She answered on the second ring.

"Have you spoken with Dr. Stanley again?" he demanded.

"Hello to you, too. I'm fine, thanks for asking."

He apologized for his rudeness. "I'm sorry, Meredith, but I don't have much time. I've got a sick mother in the clinic and questions on my mind. I need your help."

"Since I don't know nothin' about birthin' no babies, I guess you're calling me because of the questions."

He laughed. "You guess right."

"Then I'll take a chance and make a second guess that those questions involve Lauren Stanley."

"You'd be right about that, too. I think someone tried to poison her, Meredith. If I hadn't gotten to her as fast as I did, this phone call would be going a lot differently."

"Oh, my God…"

He heard the rustle of sheets and then a click, as if she'd turned on a lamp.

"What happened?"

The lab work wasn't back yet, but he gave her the details and then explained their trip to Rojo. "I can't see a correlation between Peña's death and what's going on but there has to be one. Someone wants Lauren out of here."

"Or dead."

He agreed. "There has to be a connection with her mother. Do you have any thoughts?"

He could hear a pen scratching out notes, then it stopped. She paused and he waited.

"I can think of only one link," she said.

"And that would be?"

"You."

Armando held his breath, then let it out slowly.

"You were there when the mother was killed and you saw Lauren. She grows up and comes to see you but the bridge thing happens. You rescue her, but then she gets poisoned while under your care."

"You think someone might not want me seeing her?"

"I think someone doesn't want *her* seeing you."

He understood instantly. "If I can help her figure out what really happened, then her mother's killer has a lot to lose."

"Exactly."

"But she's been in therapy for years and hasn't remembered. She truly believes her mother killed herself," he said slowly.

"Because someone *told* her that was the case. And that someone was her father—the same man who hired her psychiatrist. If you help her examine her dreams and uncover the truth, the killer would be very unhappy. He'd want her dead. And you, too, I would imagine."

"But why now? After all these years?"

"He didn't see the risk until she got there and he figured out what was going on."

There were holes but overall her logic made sense. "Have you spoken with her father?"

"Not since I told him where she was."

"He had journals about my work in his office. That's how Lauren decided I was the one who could help her."

"He couldn't have known that was you at the party that night."

"He might have seen me. They always publish photographs with the journals. Maybe he saw me at the party and later on connected my face to the picture."

"He just happened to see the journal?"

"He's a psychiatrist—he probably takes them all."

"Okay," she conceded. "Say I buy that theory, why make the mother's death a suicide?"

"Maybe he actually believed it was. He

told Lauren the press release about the burglar was put out by the State Department to protect Margaret's legacy."

"But if he killed her—"

"If he killed her, the suicide story would have been the easiest way for him to cover his tracks. No one would have known."

"J. Freeman Stanley doesn't strike me as a man who'd go for the obvious," she said. "Maybe he actually *did* think that was the case."

"The gun wasn't in her hand when I saw her."

"Then someone moved it between the time when you left and he arrived."

"Couldn't have happened."

"There were hundreds of people there that night."

"Yes, but none of them would have had the time."

"Not even Daniel Cunningham?"

Armando thought for a moment then went around the question. "I found out tonight that Lauren's father contacted him before he located you."

"That's certainly interesting…. Could the father and this Cunningham character have been working together?"

"Of course, but why?" He tapped his fingers against his desk and let his thoughts wander. They focused on an idea that he couldn't ignore. "Psychosis can be a product of trauma, which only needs to be perceived. Reality isn't always part of the picture."

"I know it's your third language, but speak English."

"Perhaps they were covering up for each other?"

Her voice turned excited. "Maybe the two of them were lovers—"

"I'd be surprised. Cunningham thought himself a ladies' man. If he *was* gay, he hid it well."

"Murder doesn't seem like a good way to handle that, in any case. I mean, why not just get a divorce, right?"

"That would be logical but logic doesn't always prevail in those kinds of circumstances, Meredith. Attractions are power-ful, minds get confused."

A long silence built as Armando got lost in the possibilities. When Meredith broke the quiet, it was clear his conclusion had sent her in a different direction.

"So is that what's going on with you and Lauren Stanley? I have the feeling there's more between the two of you than I understand. And *that* certainly wouldn't be logical…."

"You know me too well," he said rue-fully. "That is not fair."

"I'm a woman," she answered. "I don't have to play fair. Just tell me the truth and be done with it."

He didn't want to go down that path. He steered her a different way.

"I'm beginning to understand her better," he pretended to confess. "And that always brings a certain amount of closeness with it, whether we want it or not. She thinks I feel badly because of the distance between me and my family. She believes I feel guilty about it, as a matter of fact. She's wrong, but it made me see her problem more clearly." He explained the transference he'd seen and Lauren's own feelings of remorse.

"So you think she went there to make amends?" Meredith fell for the switch, her voice revealing her confusion. "For what?"

"Her mother's death."

"That doesn't make sense. She was just a kid when that happened! She didn't have anything to do with—"

"Of course she didn't, but a lot of family members of suicide victims feel they're at fault for the tragedy. It's a very typical response." He thought about what that meant for Lauren. She was living under a cloud she didn't deserve. "If I'm right, and I think that I am, then Lauren should understand she isn't responsible for that death," he said thoughtfully. "She deserves to know. It's the least I can do for her."

Meredith started to answer him but someone else spoke behind him. Still gripping the phone, Armando turned instantly.

"Who are you talking to?" Lauren demanded. "And what do I deserve to know?"

CHAPTER TEN

ARMANDO DIDN'T SEEM SURPRISED to see Lauren, nor did her questions appear to unnerve him. He spoke quietly into the phone, his gaze never leaving hers. "I have to go now. Ms. Stanley is here." He nodded several times as someone on the other end clearly continued to speak. "Yes, yes. I'll give her your regards. And thank you for your help. *Dé a mi madre un abrazo.*"

Give my mother a hug? Lauren mentally made the translation, her confusion only growing. Unable to sleep, she'd come to his office to see if she could do anything to help him with Zue's niece and instead she'd caught the end of a conversation about herself. *She deserves to know that. It's the least that I can do for her.*

He hung up the phone. "Didn't your mother teach you to knock on closed doors?"

His voice was pleasant enough but trepidation ran through her anyway.

"I touched the knob and the door swung open." She shrugged casually. "I wasn't trying to intrude but—"

"But you did."

After a moment of quiet, she met his gaze and she didn't back down. "Yes, I suppose I did. So, who *were* you talking to?"

He came from behind his desk to stand next to her. He'd cleaned up, she noticed, but he hadn't shaved. His beard had grown heavier and so had the secrets in his eyes.

"I was speaking to my father," he said. "As I told you before, he's a psychiatrist and he knows more about South American herbal remedies than I do. I wanted to know if he thought a tea made from the plant I saw today could create the symptoms I witnessed in you."

"What did he say?" She kept her voice even.

"He said it was possible. It can produce

a highly poisonous extract if it's handled properly. Not too many people know how to do that, but it's well known in the terrorist world. Unfortunately."

"What were you talking about when you said 'she deserves to know that'?"

His jaw tightened. He wasn't happy at having to explain his conversation to her. "You do not want to leave here. I needed to be sure my suspicion about the tea was correct since I was pressing you to do something you weren't in agreement with. You deserve to know the truth, regardless of how I feel."

She relaxed slightly, the tension she'd been holding in her shoulders abating with his explanation. But only somewhat. "I didn't think you were close to your father."

"I'm not. But he's a very good psychiatrist and an excellent physician. And I trust him. If he tells me something, I know it is the truth."

"I understand."

"Did you need something?" He changed

the subject abruptly. "I thought you'd gone to bed."

"I started thinking about Zue's niece. I wanted to see if there was anything I could do to help."

He seemed surprised. "I thought you said you were a don't-bleed-in-front-of-me-or-I'll-faint kind of person."

"I am, but that doesn't mean I can't do something."

"As it turns out, I don't think either one of us can do anything. She's fine. Zue's just nervous about the pregnancy. She's the one who is upset, not the mother."

"That's good. I'm glad to hear everything's going to be okay."

She waited a few seconds longer wishing she could ask him more but knowing there was no point. Had he really been speaking with his father? Lauren felt it was reasonable he would want to consult someone and she knew she should be grateful for his sense of responsibility but, at the same time, he'd been noticeably unhappy at her appearance. She couldn't think why he would lie to her, though. And who else would even care about what was happening to her?

The image of her own father's face unexpectedly came into her mind. The idea that Armando might have been talking to him made no more sense than anything else, yet Lauren couldn't help but wonder. Were the two of them conspiring to get her out of Peru? She shook the idea from her head. "I guess I'll go back to bed if you don't need me, then." She started toward the door but his voice stopped her. When she turned, he was right behind her and she hadn't even heard him move.

She took a step back and pulled her thin robe closer, the silky fabric no protection against the warmth in his eyes and the feelings that were building inside her.

"I didn't say I didn't need you."

She blinked.

"Every man needs a woman like you, Lauren."

The way he pronounced her name rooted her feet in place, the compliment rolling off his tongue with a smoothness that took away her breath. The desire she'd felt when he'd kissed her earlier roared back.

"You're a very beautiful woman," he said. "You impress me, you know."

"I do?" she asked faintly.

"Yes, you do." He lifted his hand and tucked a strand of her hair behind her ear, his fingers trailing down the side of her jaw. "I confess I have an ulterior motive in trying to get you to go home."

"What is that?"

"Your presence tempts me. I haven't been around someone like you in a very long time."

"Now you're flattering me."

"I'm telling you the truth. You're beautiful, you're smart, you're sexy…. I'm out of practice and I don't know how to deal with you."

"I don't need to be dealt with," she countered. "All I want is some help."

"And I've given you nothing."

Sensing a break in his resolution—or maybe just imagining one—she asked,

"Do you think you might change your mind about that?"

"No." His voice was sharp and decisive, then he softened it. "But if anyone *could* make me have second thoughts, it'd be you."

She swallowed her disappointment. "I guess I'll take that as a compliment, then."

He leaned over and brushed his lips across hers, lingering just long enough to let her know he'd go on if she gave him the slightest chance. When she stayed still, he pulled back. "It is definitely a compliment," he promised. "You can trust me on that."

THEY SAID THEIR GOOD-NIGHTS, and Lauren left his bungalow, Armando's stare following her until she disappeared into the darkness. He had to force his mind away from his desire, so he turned to his conversation with Meredith for refuge.

If Lauren's father was trying to have her killed, sending her back to Dallas was the last thing Armando should do. She'd be going from one bad situation to another and the inevitable would happen.

But if her father was innocent and someone local was trying to kill her, then keeping her here would be equally dangerous. There were a lot of ways to die in the jungle and none of them were pleasant. Armando knew because he'd seen them all, from one perspective or another.

He closed his eyes and cursed his dilemma, the cool air doing nothing to lessen the chaos within him.

He didn't want her here, but he couldn't send her away.

LAUREN GOT UP the next morning more confused than ever. Their trip to Rojo had taught her absolutely nothing except that Arturo Peña liked to chew coca leaves and he had poisonous plants in his front yard. She'd learned more about Armando than anything else and what she'd found out she'd suspected already; he lied when it was convenient.

She didn't know who had been on the other end of that phone last night but it hadn't been his father. She'd returned to her bed with Armando's insistence she should go back to Dallas mixing with her questions about his telephone call. The combination had kept her up for a long time. After several restless hours, she'd finally managed some sleep but her dreams had been waiting for her. She'd woken in a sweat.

After breakfast, she headed back to Armando's office. Last week, she'd spotted several books on his shelves about Machu Picchu. If she couldn't make up her mind about what to do next then maybe some research for her article would get her brain going in the right direction.

He had clinic hours scheduled for that morning, but remembering his comment from the night before, Lauren tapped on his office door. It swung open on its own once again but this time the chair behind his desk was empty. Lauren found herself relieved. The idea that someone was trying to kill her was scary enough but the feelings that she had for Armando seemed almost out of control. The more mysterious he seemed, the more intrigued she became.

What kind of self-respecting woman found herself in that kind of predicament?

She walked inside his office, then paused. All she wanted was a book or two, but some people were particular about lending from their libraries. To forestall any problems, she decided to find what she wanted and just sit down in the corner to read. Chances were good she'd be done and gone before he was finished at the clinic. She'd make sure that she was.

She stood in front of the bookcase and tried to locate the history of the ruins that had caught her eye before. Running her fingers along the spines on the first shelf, she found the book and then several others on the same topic. She pulled out half a dozen and started toward a comfortable chair located in the corner of the room, passing two more bookcases, each packed. She didn't make it past the last one. Her gaze caught another title and she stopped abruptly.

Recovered Memories of Post-traumatic Stress Victims: The Psychological Ramifications of Implantation within the Milieu of

Mental Health Therapy with Special Regard to Dream Therapy... A list of three authors' names followed. The publisher was the American Association of Psychologists.

Her arms full, she went to the chair and dropped the books on Machu Picchu on the floor. Then she returned to tilt her head and scan the other titles. All of them sounded as complex as the first one she'd noticed. Shooting a look over her shoulder, she selected two of the slimmer volumes; *Personal Memory and the Limits of Dream Recognition* and *The Potential Non-truth of the Truth Consensus Effect.* She grabbed a professional journal on dream therapy that looked promising but, reading the date stamped on its top right-hand corner, she stopped and frowned.

The report had been published two months ago. She felt her lips tighten. He might not engage in dream therapy anymore, but Armando's interest in it apparently hadn't waned.

Settling into the chair, she reached for the history guide on top of the pile, but picked up one of the books on memory instead. Two hours later, after filling half a notebook with scribbled comments and questions, she sat back in stunned disbelief, the text in her lap open to a page where a quote from the Royal University of Psychiatrists (1997) had been highlighted.

The term *recovered memory* is used to describe those recollections that are perceived to have been unavailable for a period of time. A common example of this would be the misplacement of something simple, such as keys or a book. When the memory returns it then becomes a "recovered" memory. These memories may not be accurate, however, and the use of such procedures as dream interpretation or regression therapies to aid in this process should be avoided. There is no proof they can produce accurate information about any past trauma. In fact, studies have suggested these very techniques can result in memories of events that never actually happened.

She reread the last sentence two more times then she closed her eyes, the idea jolting her. Memories could be created? How could that be? She'd always assumed her dreams held the secret to her past but what if her recollections weren't accurate?

Lauren knew that very few psychiatrists considered dream interpretation to be a legitimate addition to their therapy arsenal, but that was one of the reasons she'd sought out Armando. She'd always sensed that there were holes in her memory her regular treatment would never be able to fill, but it never crossed her mind to question the recollections themselves.

When she'd asked her father and Dr. Gladney about the problem, they had each told Lauren that subconsciously she needed to hear her mother's side of the story. Clearly that would remain missing, so there would always be gaps in her experience.

But Lauren had never accepted that

answer. Compared to other details she'd retained about that night, which were consistently sharp, her recall of her mother's death was vague and imprecise. Instead of being a witness, she often looked back on what had happened and felt as if someone had told her a story. A very bad, very tragic, life-altering story.

She'd pressured her father for a better answer. He'd lectured her as if talking to an audience of colleagues at a seminar. Memory wasn't like a VCR, he'd intoned. It didn't record impressions and sensations for later playback. People recalled bits and pieces of reality. Recollections, even of traumatic events, weren't always exact.

When she'd pressed him about her dreams, he'd had an answer for that, as well. Dreams, he'd said sternly, were not gauges of the truth. Yes, Freud had seen them as the "royal road" to the unconscious but contemporary therapists knew better. Dreams were dreams. They rehashed that which had already happened, but offered little that was new.

…In fact, studies have suggested these very techniques can result in memories of events that never actually happened.

She looked back down at the book in her lap and slowly closed it, her fingers tracing the cover.

Her father had made it sound as if there were only one explanation for her confusion, but if what she'd just read was accurate, that was not the case. There was definitely more than one reason she might feel as if segments were missing.

Memories could be manufactured.

The idea was a terrifying one and made no sense whatsoever, but if the possibility existed—and it clearly did—then why hadn't her father mentioned it?

He was well known in his field and well respected. He *taught* psychiatry. There was no way he could have been ignorant of this alternative.

Her thoughts turned to Dr. Gladney. Her father had selected the woman for Lauren and she'd been the perfect choice. She'd guided Lauren over the rocky road of her childhood and through her adolescence, even becoming a sort of substitute mother. She had an impeccable reputation and Lauren had always trusted her.

Her father was her father and he loved her. Dr. Gladney was a kind and caring doctor. Neither of them had anything but Lauren's well-being foremost in their minds. There was no way either of them could be guilty of doing anything except caring too much.

A flash of color pulled her gaze toward a rubber tree and Lauren stared out the window, her mind now in complete turmoil. On a low-hanging branch, a huge parrot preened in the hot sunshine, the light glinting off his emerald and ruby feathers. A moment later, the door to the office opened and Armando stepped in.

HE QUICKLY TOOK IN Lauren's face and the books that surrounded her chair. When he read one of the titles, he found himself holding his breath. "You discovered my library," he said after a moment.

"I hope you don't mind." Her voice sounded distant. "I saw the books on Machu Picchu and I thought they might get me started on my article."

He closed the door behind him and walked to where she sat, picking up one of the textbooks from the pile. "This isn't about the ruins."

He waited for an explanation, but she remained silent, and Armando was conflicted—once again—by his desire to help her, his desire to protect her and his desire *for* her. Meredith's remark came back to him. There definitely was something between him and Lauren, but what exactly was the "more" that Meredith had sensed and questioned him about? Armando needed a name for the feelings Lauren evoked inside him but when the answer came to him, he forced it away.

He couldn't be falling in love with Lauren.

That wouldn't work.

He kneeled beside her chair. Her eyes

were troubled as she turned to him and tapped the book he still held. "Talk to me about this," she said. "I want to understand. This thesis seems to imply that our memories aren't always…accurate."

He started to refuse. A mini-course in the study of memory would be a minefield for both of them, but it would definitely slow things down and give him some time to decide which would be better—sending her back or watching over her here.

He hedged. "You find this interesting? It's very dry reading, isn't it?"

"Nothing is boring if you think it could pertain to yourself."

He read the title, *Dream Interpretation and Memory Recovery; the Florence False Interpretation Study,* then raised his eyes to hers, the band of anxiety around his chest tightening even more. "What makes you think this applies to you?"

"Let's just say it set off some alarm bells." She studied him. "I've never heard of recovered memories. The idea troubles me."

As well it should, he thought.

"It's very complicated material," he countered.

"You said yourself I was smart. I think I can handle it."

"Being smart and accepting what this hypothesizes are two very different things." He lifted the book up. "I have no doubt you can understand the theory. My question is—do you want to? And if so, why?"

"I guess that all depends."

"On?"

"On whether or not the truth comes out."

"There's no way to tell."

"Yes, there is," she said flatly. "Once I understand what these books are saying, I'll *know* if my memories are right or not. I'll be able to tell—"

"You can't count on your feelings to judge reality—"

"I have more than my feelings, Armando." Her eyes locked on his. "I have you. You'll be my lie detector."

Armando's expression didn't shift but on the inside, he felt his world tilt. He stood. "What makes you think I can serve that purpose?"

"You're an honest man," she said. Then she added, "And I trust you."

"That trust may be misplaced."

"I don't think so."

"You don't know me that well, Lauren. I'm not the person—"

She put her hand on his arm. "Please, don't tell me you aren't the person I think you are. Some truths are better off being sensed rather than analyzed and I know which is which."

"You're depending on emotions for something that needs logic."

"You don't understand so don't even try." She gripped the book so hard that her knuckles turned white. "Just tell me what this means. Explain it to me. That's all I need for you to do."

He turned away from her pleading eyes, then, a moment later, he faced her again. "Do you realize it's Christmas eve?"

Her mouth fell open but he didn't know if her surprise came from his abrupt switch in topics or his question. "No! Is it? I…I had no idea."

"Do you still want to see the ruins?"

"Yes, but—"

"I already told Zue that I was shutting down the clinic this afternoon. Her niece will be fine for a few days. If you want to talk about this, I need to clear my head first."

"What are you suggesting?"

"Let's go to Machu Picchu," he said. "A change of scenery will do us both some good. If you feel the same way once we're there, I'll explain any theory you like."

CHAPTER ELEVEN

BEFORE SHE AND ARMANDO LEFT for their trip to the ruins, Lauren called her father and wished him a merry Christmas. The conversation was short and stilted. There were a thousand questions she wanted to ask him about what she'd read, but this wasn't the right time. Ignoring them while she made small talk wasn't easy, and she hung up as soon as she could.

She finished packing after that, tucking a few last items, including some jeans and another clean T-shirt she'd bought before they'd left Rojo into the woven bag Zue had loaned her. The cash her father had sent her went into the pocket on the side of the bag as well as the replacement passport he'd obtained and forwarded to her. Her thoughts weren't on the task at hand, though. All she could think about was what she'd read and Armando's promise to tell her more. Sandwiched between those thoughts was her ever-increasing desire for Armando, which she didn't know how to handle.

Armando materialized at the door to the ward a minute later, a small bag, similar to her own, in one of his hands. "Are you ready?"

She glanced up, her answer dying on her lips as she studied him. A pair of worn jeans were welded to his narrow hips, his T-shirt just as tight. His leather jacket had seen better days but the scratched elbows and softened cuffs made it even more appealing in her eyes. She couldn't tell which glinted more brightly in the sunshine, his black hair or the gold at his wrist. She was ready, all right, but not the way he meant.

She closed her bag and walked toward him. "How long will we be gone?"

What kind of arrangements had he made, was what she was really asking. Would they spend the night together?

"We'll catch the train at Ollantaytambo early tomorrow morning." He started for the shed and she followed. "It makes a quick stop there, then it's an hour to get to Aquas Caliente. It's not much of a town, but we can get on the bus that goes up to the ruins there. We don't need to stay at a hotel. I have friends in Ollantaytambo and Aquas."

She wondered how many bedrooms these friends had, then she put the thought aside, a silly response coming to mind to keep the images at bay.

"Trains, buses and motorcycles, huh? This is a trip that takes just about everything."

"Almost. At least it doesn't require a mule or a llama anymore. Before the road was built up the mountain, they were the only way you could go the last stretch. It's eight kilometers, but I'm sure it felt a lot longer on the back of an animal."

"Thank God for buses," she said.

"You might want to wait on giving that

thanks." They reached the barn and he pulled the doors open. "The drive up can be pretty harrowing. It narrows to a single lane in several spots but no one's told the bus drivers that. On occasion, you have to back up before you can go forward."

"Life is like that sometimes."

His smile sent a shiver of warmth down her back, then he handed her the helmet she'd worn the day before. She put it on and climbed on the bike and they set off once again.

THEY ARRIVED IN OLLANTAYTAMBO an hour or so later. Maneuvering the bike through the narrow streets, Armando drove them straight to Ruth Uvalde's home and parked, a sigh of relief escaping his lips. With Lauren's breasts warm against his back and her thighs pressing on either side of his, he'd been able to think of nothing except their kiss. He desperately wanted to repeat it and see if he'd been as affected by it as he thought he had been.

The sound of the bike's engine was still in the air when Ruth opened her front door, a grin splitting her expression. She met them halfway down the sidewalk and hugged him tightly, her welcome as large as her presence.

"Do you have room for an old friend tonight?" he asked when they parted. "And the friend of an old friend, too?" He tilted his head toward Lauren.

"Of course, I have room!" Ruth cried. "For you, always, sweetheart, always!" She motioned to Lauren to come forward and sent a sideways glance to Armando. "Who's the beauty?" she said in a pseudo-whisper. "And what's she doing with you?"

Armando laughed then introduced the two women. "This is Ruth Uvalde," he told Lauren. "She served as my nurse and right-hand man when I first opened the clinic." Turning back to Ruth he said, "And this is Lauren Stanley. I'm taking her to see the ruins. Be nice to her and don't tell her all those lies about me that you usually do, okay?"

Lauren smiled and held out her hand, but Ruth ignored her fingers and embraced her instead.

"I'll tell her what I please," the nurse announced as she released Lauren. "She'll have to decide for herself if it's the truth or not."

Armando laughed again. Ruth knew more about him than anyone but she'd kept her mouth closed for years. For that very reason, they'd been friends a long time.

She led them into her house then pointed down the hallway. "You know where to put your things," she instructed Armando. "Go get organized and Lauren and I will get to know each other."

Armando did as Ruth instructed. He came back down the hall a few minutes later.

"So then Manco gave you up and you went to the clinic…." The nurse was shaking her head as he walked back into the living room. "That old faker is so full of baloney, I can't believe he's still around. It's a miracle he didn't kill you before Armando could get there. I've always suspected there's more to

Manco than we know about but he's a character, that's for sure."

She turned as Armando sat down on the couch. "Don't get too comfortable," she warned. "I was just about to go to the market to get some things for dinner. Now you can go for me. That way I'll have more time to chat with Lauren."

"I'll take everyone out," Armando offered. "We don't want to cause you any more trouble—"

"You aren't causing me one bit of trouble. You have perfect timing, in fact. I'm having some friends over tonight anyway. I'd planned it weeks ago. You can help." She struggled up from the couch. "Let me get my shopping list. I'll be right back."

Armando turned to Lauren but, before he could say anything, Ruth hustled back into the room, her large girth moving with the grace and speed Armando had come to associate with her. She thrust a piece of paper at him. "That should do it," she said, beaming.

He glanced down and whistled. "How many people are you going to feed besides us? This amount of food could provide for a small village!"

She fluttered her hands. "Ten, twenty…something like that, I forget exactly," she replied. "Now leave us alone and don't come back until you've gotten everything on the list."

The door closed behind him and as he walked down the sidewalk, he heard Ruth's voice through the open living-room window.

"Let's go in the kitchen and we can peel apples and talk," Ruth said. "First tell me, though, what brought you here…"

Armando shook his head and took off down the street. When he came back an hour later, he found both women in the kitchen, up to their elbows in preparations. Lauren was laughing when he walked into the room.

He dropped a sack of greens on the table and a plastic bag of cans and jars on the counter beside her. "You two look like you're having way too much fun," he said. Stealing one of the carrots Lauren had been cleaning, he bit off the end as Ruth responded.

He barely heard what she said. He couldn't take his eyes off Lauren. He'd thought her stunning but she was even more beautiful when she was relaxed. How could that be?

Ruth said something about picking some tomatoes and went out to the garden. Armando found his hands on Lauren's shoulders as the door slammed shut behind the older woman.

They stood in silence while his fingers slowly massaged her muscles. After a moment, she turned within the circle of his arms and their eyes locked.

"It seems strange, doesn't it?" she asked.

He knew instantly what she meant. They'd met under circumstances like no other. He'd saved her life twice. They had nothing but uncertainty before them. Standing in a kitchen, sharing a moment this normal, felt outside the realm of their existence.

"Life isn't always predictable," he answered.

She placed her hands on his chest and her touch awoke his desire, the look in her eyes encouraging it even more.

"I don't think I want predictable any longer," she said, surprising him.

He leaned down and brushed his lips over hers, the kiss holding a promise they both understood.

"Why is that?" he murmured.

Her eyes turned into sapphires. "I like what I've found when I haven't been looking."

RUTH'S "TEN OR TWENTY" FRIENDS was close to forty. Lauren found herself grateful for the woman's hospitality and appreciative of the crowd, as well. The change in pace and people felt good, but not having to be alone with Armando was even better. Their closeness was getting to her.

Ruth took Lauren by the hand and introduced her to each of her friends, leaving Armando on his own. Everyone Lauren met seemed to have a story about him and all of them were positive. She even talked to one little girl who told her how he'd "fixed up" her kitty's broken leg.

Lauren teased him about it when they found each other late in the evening on an isolated corner of the deck. "I hear you double as a vet. I didn't know that you were so talented."

He grinned. "You met Patricia? How is Blanco?"

"He's apparently doing quite well. If you ever want a different career, they'll welcome you at the animal clinic."

"I'm happy where I am, thank you very much. I like patients who can talk." He glanced at her with approval, then nodded as if to himself.

"What?" she asked with a laugh.

"You're having fun," he said.

"Yes, I am. And it feels good."

"It does to me, too. Let me get us fresh drinks and we'll talk about why that's the case."

As he walked off, carrying their glasses, snatches of a conversation reached her ears, the talk carried on the cool night air along with the fragrant scent of the potted gardenias beside her. She glanced over her shoulder to see Ruth and a group of women talking, but their view of Lauren was blocked by the plants.

"How well do you think she knows him?" one of the women asked.

Ruth made a puffing sound. "As well as he wants her to, that's how much. Armando keeps his past where he thinks it belongs—in his past. If he's shared any of it with Lauren, I'd be very surprised."

A redhead spoke up. "I think she should know all his secrets!"

One of the other women laughed and leaned toward another one. "Yes, and I think we should, too! Ruth's been much too tight-lipped and mysterious all these years. She should tell us everything!"

The women's curiosity matched Lauren's. She leaned closer.

"His past is his past. Who he is today has nothing to do with who he was or even who he will be. Armando has always been good to me." Ruth's loyal defense was tinged with stubbornness. "I'd still be working with him if it weren't for my hip. He's a good man. A fine man. Nothing else matters."

The sound of their voices dropped after that and Lauren realized she wasn't going to be able to hear unless she followed. She was moving toward them when Armando appeared at her side.

"What's going on?"

"No-nothing," she stuttered. "I was just—"

"Eavesdropping?" He supplied the word as he handed her a drink.

She blushed, her face turning warm. "I didn't mean to—"

"Of course, you did," he said. "Your ears were practically rotating." He threw the women another glance. "What kind of nonsense were they talking about?"

When she didn't answer, he shook his head. "Let me guess, then. You? Me? Both of us?"

She framed her answer carefully. "Everyone enjoys idle gossip, Armando. It's harmless. They didn't mean anything by it.

People like to make up stories when they don't know the truth."

"Why?" he asked. "Who cares?"

"You should know. It's human nature."

Inside the house someone laughed loudly and then a stereo began to play. As the music filled the air around them, people began to dance.

Placing his beer on the railing behind Lauren, Armando took her in his arms, his ploy to distract her obvious.

"I have to admit I've been wondering myself." She leaned back slightly. "The articles I read about you never explained why you dropped out of sight after med school."

"We've been over this already."

"That's true," she agreed. "But you didn't answer me, remember?"

"Discussing this is pointless." He slid his hands down her back and pulled her closer. "I've said all I'm going to so don't ask me any more."

His touch was sizzling yet his manner was abrupt and cold; she was instantly more curious than ever before. One look at his expression, though, and she knew better than to press him. The subject stayed on her mind, however, even after everyone left and they all went to bed. Each, it turned out, in a separate bedroom. Climbing between the sheets, Lauren vowed she'd catch Ruth alone the next morning and confront her with what she'd overheard. Maybe the nurse would tell her more.

As usual, things didn't work out as she'd planned. Armando got Lauren up and they were out the door before their hostess was even awake. After buying some supplies for the trip, they then went directly to the station. Twenty minutes after that, they were on the train to Aquas Caliente. His aloof attitude remained.

The seats were really just padded benches but their car was almost empty. Tourist season ran through July and August; the historical ruins apparently weren't a popular Christmas destination. They protected their cups of maté against the motion of the train as it pulled out of the station. Ollantaytambo lay on the edge of the Urubamba Valley and, within moments, the train was speeding past a lush green landscape bisected by ancient stone walls. Mist-covered mountains shimmered in the distance, the rushing Urubamba River flowing beside the tracks. Lauren turned to Armando but the noise of the train made conversation impossible and in the end she was glad. By the time they reached Aquas Caliente a short time later, he seemed to have thawed.

Stepping off the train station, he took her elbow as they were mobbed by T-shirt vendors and women hawking tapes of Peruvian music. Lauren felt disappointment over the frantic commercialism, but then she put it into perspective. The people around her were merely trying to make a living, just like the people who'd inhabited the area so long ago. Armando guided her through the crowd.

"This way," he said, tilting his head to his left. "We can walk to my friend's home and rest for a bit. We'll take the bus that goes to the ruins after lunch."

As soon as they headed down a side street, everything changed. The air lost its sooty smell and was replaced with a fresh clean breeze. Mud huts and thatched roofs were substituted for the brick-and-tiled station buildings and children instead of vendors talked loudly in the streets. A Peruvian version of "Jingle Bells" slipped out an open window. In five minutes, they were standing beside a wooden gate with a small window cut in the center. Through the filigreed iron grate that covered it, Lauren could see a stuccoed home. As Armando rang the bell set in the post beside them, she could hear its echo inside the house.

No one came. He gave the button another long push, then he leaned over and moved a flower pot heavy with red poppies. A key glinted in the dirt left behind.

"My friends travel a lot," he explained. "I'm not surprised they're gone. They're both retired doctors and they have a son with grandchildren in Lima, so they probably went there for the holidays."

"It's okay?" she asked as he unlocked the gate.

"Absolutely. If they found out I came and stayed anywhere else, they'd be offended. The Bustamantes—Kioto and Salvina—and my family go way back. They're contemporaries of my parents."

He opened the inner door and they stepped inside a small entry. To the left was a hallway with stairs, to the right, a living room filled with sunlight from high-set windows. Beyond it was a kitchen that looked out to a courtyard.

"Give me your bag," Armando instructed, "and I'll take everything upstairs." He pointed toward the kitchen. "I'm sure they have tea if you'd like to make some."

She did as he instructed, feelingly slightly uncomfortable looking through the cabinets of a stranger's house but finding cups and saucers, milk and sugar. By the time he was back, the pot was boiling.

They took their mugs and went outside, the sun warm, the quiet soothing. Lauren closed her eyes and tried not to think but, after a while, she had to break the silence. The time had come.

She looked at him. "Talk to me," she said quietly. "Tell me about what I read."

"WHAT EXACTLY IS IT that you want to know?" he asked. His voice was guarded. "The books you picked out cover a pretty wide range of experiences."

A determined look came over her features. "I want to know everything," she replied. "But I want to start with a certain term that was used about memories. I'd never heard of it before and certainly not in reference to dream therapy."

"What was it?"

"In the study I read, they called it *FMS*."

Lauren was a smart woman; she'd gone straight to the heart of the matter. *"False Memory Syndrome."*

She leaned toward him, her eyes probing. "What is that, Armando?"

"FMS is a condition in which a person's belief in something is so strong that it dominates his identity and personality. In reality, though, the thing he believes in never actually happened. It's a very destructive disorder because it's almost impossible to prove—or disprove—a real memory from a false one."

"I thought traumatic memories were *better* remembered than any other kind. Aren't they supposed to be more accurate?"

"A lot of people believe that, but it is not the truth. Stressful memories are subject to the same forces everyday memories are— misunderstanding, decay, change, distortion. Our past continually rewrites itself."

"How do dreams play into this?"

"They're open to misunderstanding, too. That's what the Florence study proved."

"Give it to me in layman's terms."

"The study involved therapists who interpreted dreams for different people but no matter what the dream was about, the clinician told the patient it meant they'd been lost as a child. This was reinforced several times and by the end of the study, the majority of the participants believed they'd gotten lost once despite the fact they'd reported beforehand that had never happened to them."

"How can someone convince themselves something happened to them when it didn't?"

"Suggestion is a powerful tool," he answered, then added, "especially in the hands of an authority figure like a doctor or a therapist. People seeking help want to find it…so they believe."

She nodded slowly. "I've thought if I could understand my nightmares, I could understand what had happened. I came this far to see you. I guess I can see that."

"Dreams are important, but they won't unlock the door to your past. If that's what you are looking for, you couldn't be more wrong."

"I'm not sure what I'm looking for now," she said. "The goal line's moved."

"How so?"

"This whole thing about recovered memories bothers me. I wanted to read about dreams but when I saw that study, it stopped me completely."

He spoke carefully. "Do you feel your memories of that night are inaccurate?"

"I think they must be," she answered. "According to everything I read in your office, no one's memory is precise."

"That's true."

"I never doubted what I recalled, but there were times when things didn't seem right." She told him the details she retained from the party. When she got to the point when she mentioned Daniel Cunningham, Armando found himself tensing, his body rigid as she described the attaché he'd been standing beside that night. She moved on quickly, however, and said nothing about Armando.

"After that, everything gets kind of blurry, like I'm looking through a window with curtains over it." She shook her head. "I don't understand how I can remember the music and my mother's dress and the decorations so vividly yet when it comes to seeing her pull the trigger, I go blank. The next thing I recall is my father picking me up."

He'd been holding his breath as she talked. When she finished, Armando let it out softly. "False memories *are* vague and undefined," he said, "but real ones can be, too." He paused to frame his query. "You *did* see the gun, though?"

"Oh, yeah. I remember the gun. She was holding it. Her fingers were curled around the trigger. She'd had her nails done for the party and the red polish matched her dress. I definitely remember that."

"Was that before or after your father took you in his arms?"

Lost in her memory, she answered without thinking. "During," she said. "I was looking at her over his shoulder."

"You must have felt awful. Was your father crying and upset, too? Can you remember his face when he came in?"

"No," she said. "I was looking at her when he opened the door. But I heard him say, 'Oh, my God, Margaret!' He kneeled down and reached out—I guess he was checking her pulse. I couldn't tell because his body was between us, then he stood up and came to where I was."

"So you remember hiding in the closet,

then the next thing you recall is coming out and seeing her. Your father came in, checked her and picked you up. You then saw her fingers around the gun?"

"Yes." She spoke blankly, unaware of the motivation behind his questions.

Armando reached for his cup and held it with both hands. Lauren had absolutely no memory of his presence that night. The photograph she'd seen in the psychiatric journal had triggered an understandable response but she hadn't made the connection. It was incredible, he thought, what the mind could do.

"He heard me crying out," she said quietly. "That's why he came."

She *had* been screaming when he'd left and now she'd told him that when her father had entered the room she'd still been screaming. Just as he'd told Meredith, no one could have possibly had the time to come in after him to move that gun into Margaret Stanley's hand. If someone had, Lauren would have seen him—a fact she might not remember now, but who would have known that then?

J. Freeman Stanley had to have put the weapon in his wife's hand before he'd comforted his daughter. Then he'd told her—and everyone else—that Margaret had shot herself.

But why?

Lauren's eyes were troubled when they met his. "My mother died that night. She's gone. I didn't make up any of that but I know something isn't right. Could it be my memories that are wrong?" She unknowingly repeated his own question. "And if they are, why? Why would someone plant false memories in my mind about that night?"

"I'd like to know the answer to that question myself."

She looked as if she wanted to cry but wouldn't let herself. "I always thought that my dreams were what bothered me most about that night but I think I've been wrong." She paused. "My nightmares aren't what's important here. My memories are," she said. "And now I can't trust them, either."

CHAPTER TWELVE

THERE WASN'T MUCH MORE either one of them could say after that. Armando tried to comfort her but his reassurances sounded forced. She wondered if she was imagining it, then wondered why she'd even think that. An hour later, they walked back to the center of town to catch the bus.

It roared to a stop in front them, a cloud of fine dust and the squeal of brakes accompanying its arrival. Along with a small group of German tourists, they boarded the vehicle, found two seats and sat down.

Lauren hardly knew where she was. Everything that Armando had told her sounded logical but, at the same time, it didn't. Her memory of her mother's suicide had to be accurate, she'd tell herself in one breath, and then in the next, she'd question it. How could she remember some points and go blank on others? What was behind her feelings of uncertainty? Dr. Gladney was the only therapist she'd ever seen and there was absolutely no reason for the woman to suggest anything untrue about that night to Lauren.

The bus turned right and started up the mountainside, their few fellow passengers jabbering excitedly as Lauren sat in thoughtful silence, Armando at her side. He seemed edgy and restless, his expression guarded. His glances were so subtle no one except Lauren could have caught them, but several times she saw him looking over his shoulder at the others.

Once again, she sensed he was holding back, but she didn't know why she felt that way or even what he might be keeping from her, the answers to those questions as remote as the ones puzzling her about her past. After a while, he seemed to settle down, but she wasn't sure he hadn't become aware of her notice and had begun to better hide his uneasiness.

The bus climbed higher and higher, the road narrowing as they gained altitude, the luxuriant greenery moving closer to the windows with every turn. Armando hadn't lied to her. At one point, they sped around a blind corner and the driver slammed on his brakes, alarming the passengers as he put the bus into reverse and backed down several hundred feet. The tires brushed perilously close to the edge of the road as the nose of the bus they'd unexpectedly met bumped their own. Their driver laughing all the way, they finally reached a point where the oncoming bus could pass them. A universal sigh of relief rippled through the passengers and then they were heading forward once more, the switchbacks becoming even trickier.

An hour after they'd boarded, the bus pulled into a staging area. Another vehicle passed them going down, Lauren noted, but their bus was the last one to arrive. Their group would be the final tour for the night. They paid for their tickets, then joined a man waiting at the end of a short path. He was their guide, he explained, but when his lecture was done, they were free to wander about on their own.

"Don't miss your departure, though," he warned. "No more buses will come until the morning and if you do not have reservations already at the hotel here, you will spend a cold night on the ground."

Lauren shivered at the image but not because of the obvious. A strange sensation had begun to envelope her, a coldness, and she had no idea why. When they rounded the corner and the ancient city came into view, Lauren understood her feelings. "Oh, my God…"

Armando stopped at her side and smiled, his anxiety gone. "It *is* breathtaking, isn't it?"

All she could do was nod.

A valley lay before them. It was covered in low-lying clouds that obscured the surrounding peaks. In the center was a huge plaza with thatch-covered huts on either side, their stone walls so well integrated with the landscape, it seemed as if they'd sprung up on their own. Lauren's gaze skipped randomly over the incredible sight, taking in the towering mountains with their terraced sides, the stone channels used to conduct water, the towers with small triangular windows.... She didn't know what to look at first.

"Let's catch up with the guide," Armando suggested, his hand on her elbow.

The man was already speaking when they topped the first set of stairs. "Not sure when it was built," he was saying, "but it was probably finished during the period between 1460 and 1470 by Pachacuti Inca Yupanqui, a local Inca leader. The compound was used primarily as a retreat for the religious and the royal. At one time, it's believed some eleven hundred to twelve hundred people lived here, most of them women, children and priests. There are approximately two hundred homes, palaces and temples, all of them built with rocks that fit perfectly without mortar. Some of these stones have over thirty corners and weigh over fifty tons each." He pointed toward the steppes below. "We're at an altitude of 9,060 feet. They farmed, performed ceremonies and tried to live in peace. No one knows for sure when the area was abandoned or even why, but by 1527 the Spanish explorer Pizarro had arrived in Peru. With him came the smallpox. Fifty percent of the Inca population was destroyed by the disease. Civil wars followed. Cuzco itself was seized in 1534 and many of the buildings there that had the same architecture were destroyed. Now if you'll follow me this way…"

They trailed behind the man, but paused to peer out one of the trapezoidal windows set in a thick stone wall. The day had turned warm. Armando looked briefly at the view then turned and took off his jacket, his eyes flitting over the crowd behind them.

The guide switched his topic to the American, Hiram Bingham, who'd discovered the ruins in 1911. He'd been looking for

Vilcabamba, the last stronghold of the Incas, but he'd found Machu Picchu instead.

Lauren looked at Armando. "Do you think he was disappointed?" she asked. "Bingham, I mean?"

He seemed distracted and it took him a moment to focus. "I don't see how he could have been, but I suppose it's possible. Explorers probably get tunnel vision as readily as the rest of us."

She stared out the window. Huayna Picchu, the "young peak," was right before them. She could almost hear the sound of flutes and the cries of children. The feeling was eerie.

When they caught up with the group again, they were standing beside a column of stone set in a huge slab of rounded masonry. Armando's gaze shifted across the crowd again and Lauren began to worry. He was looking for someone or something, but what? She took a second to glance around but she saw no one who looked out of the ordinary. The tourists all had their cameras slung over their shoulders and carried backpacks bulging with travel guides. She attributed her anxiety to where they were.

"This is the *intihuatana,* or the Saywa stone as it's sometimes known," the guide explained. "Rumor has it this was the site of some human sacrifices, but in reality, the priests used this area to gauge the position of the sun, especially during the two equinoxes. On March 21 and again on September 21, this stone casts no shadow when the sun is directly above it. It's also called the "Hitching Post of the Sun" because of that. Most of their religious practices were based on the position of the planets, so where the sun was located within the heavens was of primary importance. If they performed their rites at the wrong time, then their prayers would not be answered, and they might actually anger the gods instead. Beneath this area was the cemetery of Machu Picchu. Only a few mummies were discovered."

They walked another hour, marveling at the stonework and the endurance of the people who had lived in the ruins. When the guide finished, they still had time, as he'd promised, to explore on their own.

Armando let Lauren decide where to go next. "I can come any time," he explained. "You may not get back here. What would you like to look at again?"

His comment disturbed her. The thought of never seeing these magnificent ruins again hurt. She was developing an affinity for the country she'd left so abruptly so many years before. She amended the thought automatically. She wasn't *developing* the closeness—it'd been there all along and she'd been denying it. Peru seemed more like home than Dallas did. She felt more comfortable—more *at peace*—here than she ever had in Texas. The insight must have shown on her face.

"What is it?" Armando touched her arm gently. "You look surprised by something."

"I am." She sat down on one of the steps. The Germans had left and they were alone as Armando sprawled on the grass beside her.

"I just realized how good I feel here. It's strange."

"Maybe it's the elevation."

"I don't think so," she said.

"Then what?"

"I don't know," she answered slowly. "I just feel different somehow. Calmer, maybe?"

"You're not getting enough oxygen. That happens up here. Breathe less. You'll feel better."

She punched him on the shoulder, his teasing a welcome change from the heavier subjects that had weighed on her mind. "What kind of doctor are you? That doesn't sound like very good medical advice to me."

His expression turned warm and then sensual. "It probably isn't," he said, leaning toward her. "Maybe I need to do an examination so I can say for sure."

"Will that fix my problem?" she asked faintly.

"It depends," he said. "But if you let me kiss you, you'll feel so much better, you won't really care."

HE PROCEEDED TO DO just that, his lips pressing gently down on Lauren's, his hands on her arms to bring her nearer. She moved into his embrace without hesitation, her mouth parting to accept his tongue.

They'd kissed before, but there was something different about this one. Armando sensed the change and so did Lauren, or so it seemed to him. She murmured something unintelligible and clutched at his shoulders, a tension in her grip that hadn't been there before.

He could have made the kiss last forever, but Armando pulled back. He didn't want to let his guard down for long. A man on the bus had grabbed his attention from the outset and he wasn't going to relax now. The man's gaze had landed on Armando's once. He'd obviously thought Armando hadn't been watching. He'd misjudged.

Armando was always watching.

And what he *hadn't* seen had definitely bothered him. Tourists constantly checked their cameras, changed settings or looked at the photos they'd just snapped. This man had taken some shots before boarding the bus but that was all. He hadn't looked at them later or examined his camera—he'd done nothing but hit the shutter. He was traveling alone, too, and that was unusual. Backpackers always seemed to hook up with someone along the trail.

But there was something more about the blond man that bothered Armando. He seemed vaguely familiar, but Armando couldn't place him. The square jaw, the pale blue eyes, the shaggy hair. He had the nagging feeling he'd seen the man somewhere else.

But he'd wandered off with the others and now they were alone.

Armando returned his attention to Lauren, her beauty striking him so freshly, he spoke before thinking. "I don't know what it is," he confessed, "but you've captured me, Lauren. Completely. How did that happen?"

"I didn't mean to," she said. "But if it's any consolation, you've done the same to me. In fact, you did it to me before we ever met."

A catch formed in his throat. "What do you mean?"

She slipped a hand under his hair, her fingers warm and soft. "When I saw that photograph of you in my father's office…" She licked her lips. "I didn't want to tell you this earlier, but I thought my heart stopped when I saw it."

He wasn't sure he could speak, but he managed. "What do you mean?"

"I can't explain it without sounding crazy."

"Go ahead."

"I felt like I already knew you," she whispered. "I felt as if we'd met before and connected in some kind of life-altering way." She made a dismissive noise. "I know it sounds ridiculous but—"

"Nothing like that is ridiculous. Past life, dream life, future life… Who knows all the possibilities? We certainly don't. I can't say they do not exist."

"You believe me?" She seemed surprised.

"What's not to believe? Once upon a time, I felt that way myself."

"About a woman you knew?"

"About a girl who grew up to be a woman."

"Ahhh," she said. "Your first love. They're always very special. Did she feel the same for you?"

"She did. But she didn't know it at the time."

Curiosity sparked in her eyes, but she kept her questions to herself. He'd cut her off too many times; she knew she'd get no answer. She brought her hand around to his jaw and cupped it, her thumb rubbing his chin. "Her loss," she said quietly.

They kissed again then stood, their arms around each other, the valley spread below. When they returned to the bus, the sun had moved behind the mountain.

By the time they got back to the house, it was dark.

They walked inside the entry, and Armando closed the door behind them. Lauren took one step into the hallway but hesitated before going farther. When he came up behind her and put his hands on her shoulders, she turned slowly and their eyes met with a passion that rocked him.

He told himself he should stop before it was too late, but even as he thought that, he knew he wouldn't.

He began to unbutton her blouse, taking his time, their eyes never parting. Lauren stood still and seemed to hold her breath. When he finished and the blouse fell open, he eased his hands beneath the collar and pushed the garment off her shoulders. It fell to the floor with a sigh and she waited before him, two scraps of lace covering her breasts. A moment later, he had her belt undone and her pants followed. She stepped out of them and kicked them to one side, her hands reaching for his shirt before he could do anything else.

For two heartbeats, they stood before each other in silence, then Armando pulled her into his arms and carried her upstairs.

LAUREN HAD HAD OTHER LOVERS. In college, she'd even had a serious relationship she'd thought would lead to marriage before she'd realized how wrong they'd been for one another. She'd been more selective after that, but none of her encounters had prepared her for what happened next.

Armando put her on the bed and then made love to every inch of her body. Murmuring all the while, he kissed her slowly, his lips lingering in unexpected places, skipping over others, coming back twice to some. She wanted him to stop—begged him to several times—but when he did, she held her breath, then pleaded with him to continue. The more he touched her, the more she wanted him. Her need built until it was almost painful.

Finally, he lifted his face to hers and kissed her deeply…. Then he started all over again. By the time he finished, she was weak.

He pulled her on top of him and wrapped her in his arms, his hands sliding down her back, the evidence of his desire pressing between them. She buried her face in his neck, her lips finding a spot behind his neck where she nibbled at his skin.

He groaned loudly and rolled them both

over. She heard him open a drawer and the crinkling of a packet. His body poised over hers, he entered her swiftly, and they were both consumed by the passion they'd been holding back.

She wrapped her legs around him and cried his name. He cradled her in his arms and called her *mi amor.* The world tilted for both of them and then they were lost.

THEY MADE LOVE AGAIN, Armando's desire for Lauren even greater the second time. He'd established the ebb and flow of their rhythm but when she took over, she changed them. He wondered if he would ever tire of her ivory skin and sweet perfume, but he lost his thoughts as her hands slid gently over his body. There was an innocence about her that surprised him, but at the same time, an inherent sexiness that threatened to stop his heart. He knew he'd never find another woman like her and he knew that with certainty.

So what was he going to do about it?

They couldn't pretend as if life were

normal. Someone was trying to kill her and Armando was beginning to think he knew who. The more she'd talked about memories, the clearer her past had seemed.

No one but her father could have altered the crime scene. And no one but a killer had a reason for doing that.

He turned his head against the pillow where he lay and watched Lauren sleep. Should he tell her what he thought? How would she take it? It was entirely possible she might remember the whole event at some point, dredging up details that had been pushed aside, including his own presence. Anything could trigger a recall. When there were truths mixed in with untruths, it was more difficult for the victim to distinguish between the two, but not impossible. Without independent external proof, though, she would never know. The killer was the only other witness and if that was J. Freeman Stanley, he'd never offer up proof.

As that final thought formed, however, Armando realized he was wrong.

There *was* another person who could prove what had really happened that night and that person was him.

To explain that to Lauren meant a sacrifice he wasn't sure he could make.

WHEN LAUREN WOKE, she didn't know where she was. In the darkness, the room's details were indistinguishable and for a second—one single second—she was ten years old again and hiding in her mother's closet. She blinked and her moment of panic passed, but she felt foolish as she looked over to where Armando lay. He was sound asleep and she was glad he hadn't witnessed it.

Raising up on one elbow, Lauren stared at his profile. Ruth was right; he *was* an incredible man. In too many ways to count. He did have secrets, though, and Lauren wondered just how deep they went. Sometimes she felt as if she'd known him forever, but at other times he seemed like a total stranger. And what about the past he refused to discuss? *Was* he an assassin?

The idea was so at odds with the genuineness she'd seen in his eyes that she couldn't even begin to justify the two wildly divergent impressions.

But what did it matter?

In a matter of days, she'd probably be returning to Dallas and he would stay right here. He was too committed to his work and the people he helped to go anywhere else. What they'd shared this night was only temporary.

She slipped out of the bed and reached for her bag. Digging out one of her T-shirts, she pulled it over her head and tugged on some jeans, then she padded barefoot from the room, closing the door behind herself.

Once downstairs, she went into the kitchen and opened the refrigerator to grab one of the bottles of water she'd seen before. Unscrewing the top, she wandered into the living room and to the bookcases that lined one wall.

The Bustamantes were widely read people, it seemed. The cases were filled with medical texts, popular novels, religious journals. In a way, the variety reminded her of Armando's office. She looked a bit closer and realized some of the psychiatric reference books were even the same. When she pulled one out and saw Kioto Bustamante's name on the spine, she realized why.

As she put her hand on the bookcase to replace the book, the shelf moved slightly and a silver frame on the shelf above toppled over. Cursing quietly, Lauren righted the frame. Curiosity hit her, though, and she picked up the frame and brought it closer.

It took a moment for the image to soak into her brain.

When it did, a paralysis took control of her limbs and her lungs. She didn't blink, she didn't think, she didn't do anything but stare.

There were two men and a woman in the picture, all of them dressed formally. The couple, their arms wrapped around each other's waists, were a generation older than the other man. In the background, Laura could see the curve of a staircase with iron balusters. A Christmas tree glowed in the center and there was ivy wrapped around the filigree handrail. In a careless scrawl someone had scribbled the date at the bottom of the print.

Christmas Eve. 1989.

Her mind went numb. The young man looked to be in his twenties. He wore a black tuxedo, his eyes gleaming, his hair slicked back. He had his hands at his side, but his sleeve was pulled up an inch or so. On his wrist rested a heavy gold bracelet.

Lauren closed her eyes and tried to take a breath but there was no air in the room. It was gone and so was her mind. She opened her eyes once more and stared but nothing in the photograph had changed.

CHAPTER THIRTEEN

"WHAT ARE YOU DOING?"

Armando's question sliced open the silence and Lauren turned, something clutched in her hands.

Her face held the warmth of a marble bust and her eyes were huge with fear. She was trembling, he realized, and speechless.

She crossed the room in two steps and thrust a silver frame toward him.

"It was on the shelf," she said shakily, pointing to the bookcase. "Back there. I was replacing a book and it fell…."

Armando cursed. He should have checked the house before bringing her in. He'd been there so many times, the home had become like his own and he'd grown inured to the items that filled it. Now he was about to pay the price for his carelessness.

"Those are the Bustamantes," he said pointlessly. "And me."

"It was taken sixteen years ago. Almost sixteen years ago *to the day*. At the Embassy."

"Yes."

"The night my mother died."

"I know."

"No, you don't," she replied. "You don't know anything about it. But you should, shouldn't you?"

"Lauren, please—" Armando reached for her, but she jumped back.

"Don't touch me," she said, her voice cracking. "Don't even think about touching me." She shook her head, the pale strands of her hair brushing her shoulders. "You were there that night and you never bothered to tell me?"

He started to deny her accusation, but he knew how useless that would be. She held the proof in her hand.

"Sit down," he said. "Sit down and calm down and I'll explain everything."

She followed his order only, Armando suspected, because she couldn't force her legs to support herself another moment. Clutching the photograph, she sank into the couch cushions.

Armando stared at her in silence. He'd wanted to keep his past secret, but he should have known better. The truth always came out. "Take a deep breath," he said.

"I don't need a deep breath," she said. "I need the truth. And you have it."

"Not all of it."

"More than I do."

"Maybe." He hesitated. "Maybe not."

She stared at him. "Just tell me."

"I *was* there that night," he said. "I met Daniel Cunningham playing squash and he invited me. I had no idea the Bustamantes were going to be at the party, too. When they saw me, they insisted on a picture."

Lauren's expression eased. The relief of knowing this one simple fact—obvious in black and white—was written across her face. Anger quickly replaced the former emotion, however, as the truth sank in.

"Why didn't you say something before?" she asked. "All this time, we could have at least been comparing notes about that night—"

"The knowledge would not have done anything for you." He stuffed his hands into the pockets of his pants. "I knew you'd only have more questions."

"But you could have helped me answer them!"

"I can't and even if I could, they wouldn't matter."

"Why not?"

"Because history can't be rewritten, Lauren. Nothing will change that night's outcome. Your mother won't come back. And your life will *still* be in danger because of her death."

"Because of her death?" She repeated his accusation as if it would help her make sense of it. "You think someone's trying to harm me because of my mother's suicide?"

"I think her death and the attempts on

your life are linked, yes." He spoke cautiously, but the distinction he made went unnoticed. She was too upset to notice the difference between *death* and *suicide*.

"My mother killed herself and I came here to try and get some closure. No one but me would even care about that."

"Are you sure? What about your father? He seems to care."

"Because he loves me," she argued.

Armando took her hands in his, his heart torn in two as his dilemma swept over him again. If he helped her, she'd suspect him of killing her mother, but if he didn't, he might lose her completely. There was only one way to settle the problem, he decided suddenly, and that was to risk it all.

He gripped her fingers painfully. "You came here to better understand your dreams. Do you still want my assistance with that?"

She blinked in confusion. "What has that got to do with this—"

"Do you want the truth, Lauren?"

She looked at him, her eyes two wells of bewilderment and mistrust. "Yes."

"Then I'll help you," he said, "but afterward, things will be…different."

She seemed to take a mental step back. "What are you saying? Are you telling me I won't be able to handle the truth?"

"I'm saying it won't be easy."

She didn't think twice. "When can we start?" was all she said.

LAUREN COULDN'T BELIEVE what she was about to do. Armando had lied to her—out and out lied—but she was still so desperate to learn more about her past, she was willing to open up to him again, this time with her dreams. She questioned her actions yet, at the same time, in the center of her heart, she knew she was doing the right thing. She had no other choice because she trusted him.

She shouldn't.

But she did.

He made her stretch out on the couch and he covered her with a blanket. His movements were tender and considerate. When he kneeled beside the couch and cupped one hand around her cheek, his expression was full of compassion. "This isn't something I should be doing," he said. "I just want you to know that before we get started."

"I know," she said. "I know. You don't believe in it and you think it's a mistake."

"That's not why," he said softly.

"Then what is it?"

"I care for you, Lauren." He licked his lips. "I care for you a lot. Good doctors don't mix therapy and love."

She felt joy at his admission, and she hated herself for it. "Is that what's between us, Armando? Is it love?"

"What do you think?"

"I think it might be. But that scares me, too."

He brought her hands to his lips and kissed them, first one then the other. "Whatever we call it, just remember, you aren't in this alone. We'll work it out together. I'll help you, I promise."

Her eyes welled with tears. He stood and moved to the chair behind the couch. A steady silence built between them. When he broke it after a moment, his voice was quiet and soothing.

"I want you to close your eyes," he said. "I am not going to hypnotize you but I am going to relax you. Once you are feeling comfortable, then we'll start to talk."

She murmured her assent and he spoke again, repeating himself. "I want you to close your eyes and breathe until you can pull in nothing more. Fill your lungs, then exhale through your mouth. When you take your next breath, I want it to come from the top of your chest. You should feel your breasts move. Inhale, then let it out slowly."

He had her repeat the process three more times. "I want you to continue breathing in and out but this time, force the air to come from the middle of your chest. Breathe with concentration. Your rib cage should go up and down. Focus on your center."

Just as before, he had her do this several more times, then he said, "I want you to feel the air come from a different place now, farther down inside you. Your stomach should rise as you breathe.

You're lifting it up and letting it down, slowly, in and out. When you exhale, your stomach collapses. When you inhale, it expands. Breathe in, let it out. Breathe in and let it out."

As she followed his instructions, a lethargy came over Lauren. Her limbs felt heavy and unwieldy, and if he'd told her to rise and walk she wasn't sure she'd have been able to.

"Continue to breathe," he intoned, "but I want you to start at the top of your chest, then go to the middle, then finish with your stomach. The breath you take will be all-encompassing and fulfilling. I want you to hold it as long as you can, then let it out slowly. I want to hear you exhale.

"Can you hear your heart?" he asked as her sigh filled the room. "Listen closely. Listen to the pulse of your blood through your body." His voice took on a singsong rhythm. "Lie still and let your senses open up totally. I want you to feel the heat of your skin. I want you to hear the sound of your heart. I want you to smell the fragrance of your skin. Become aware of everything that's happening within you."

A sense of peace and tranquility replaced her earlier stupor. If she'd been more aware of what was going on, she would have been shocked. Instead, all she felt was a sensation of weightlessness.

"I want you to stay focused and serene," Armando said quietly. "Take one last breath, then tell me about your dream."

She did as he instructed, her voice low and monotonous. "I'm in the closet where I hid that night," she started. "The doors open by themselves and I see my mother lying on the floor. Her dress is sparkling and there's a bright red rose on the carpet, right beside her head."

As she spoke, she realized she'd started to breathe faster. She slowed down and started again. "A crow flies in the window. His feathers are black and shiny and his eyes are gold. He has a white ring around his throat."

"Who else is there?"

"At this point, no one. It's just me and

my mother and the crow. He picks up the rose beside her head and then he starts to leave but before he does, he turns into a different animal, something furry and small. He takes the rose and leaves. After that my father appears."

"What does he do?"

"Nothing," she said. "He just stands there. He sees me crying but he doesn't do anything."

A long silence built. Lauren knew Armando was waiting for more but there was nothing else. She was vaguely conscious of tears running down her cheeks yet she couldn't stop them.

"What happens after that?"

"It's all disjointed then. A blond man shows up. He has a gun. Sometimes he just disappears. After I fell off the bridge, I began to dream that he shot the rope out from beneath me."

Armando made no comment. After a moment, he said, "Tell me again about the night your mother died. You were ten years old...."

"I was ten years old," she repeated, her breathing becoming slow and regular once more. "I was excited about the party and she let me pick out her gown."

"What color was it?"

She smiled. "It was red with tiny beads all over it. I thought she looked like a movie star."

"Did you watch her get ready?"

"I did," Lauren said. "I helped her with her makeup and then her hair. She put me to bed but after the party started I got up and looked at everyone through the balusters."

"Who did you see?"

"I saw Daniel first. I had a crush on him." She described his tuxedo, then spoke of waving to him. She stopped for a moment before continuing. "There was a man standing beside him," she said. She didn't move, but she drew in an audible breath.

"Who was it?"

"It was you!"

She started to rise but he leaned over and put his hand on her shoulder, gently forcing her back down. "Relax and tell me what you saw."

She did as he suggested. "I saw you right beside him! I didn't know who you were and you scared me. I—I ran to my mother's closet and hid."

His demeanor stayed calm. "What happened after that?"

"I went to sleep. When I woke up, I heard people talking."

"What were they talking about?"

She started to say she didn't know, then she stopped. She'd never remembered this before. She inhaled slowly, the answer coming to her. "The man spoke first and he cursed. He said something like 'dammit,' then he started talking about money. My mother said she wasn't there for the money. She said, 'I love my country.'"

"Is that all?"

"No. She said, 'You aren't going to get away with this. I found out and others will, too.' Then the man said, 'They won't if you aren't talking.'"

Lauren blinked. "I— I'd forgotten I'd

heard all that. I can't believe I'm remembering it now."

"Who was he?"

He waited but she said nothing else. "Repeat the conversation."

She did but nothing else came to her. She shook her head in frustration. "I don't know who he was."

"That's fine," he said. "Go on."

"He told her not to be stupid, then I heard a sound."

"What kind of sound?"

Lauren's mouth went dry. Her stomach took a dive and she shuddered. "It was a popping sound."

"What do you think it was?"

She tried to take a breath but something seemed to be sitting on her chest. "I can't…" She clenched the blanket that covered her, a fistful of the fabric bunching in both of her hands.

"Exhale," he said. "Slowly. Then breathe again."

"It was a gunshot," she said as the air left her lungs. "I heard the gun go off."

"Then what did you do?"

"I crawled to the back of the closet and hid," she said. "I stayed there as long as I could."

"Then?"

"Then I opened the door."

"What did you see?"

"My mother." Behind Lauren's closed eyes, the image came to life. Her mother's body lay before her. A man on one knee knelt over her. He was dressed in black and even his face was covered. Lauren had never had a memory of anyone being there before this, except her father. She felt faint and almost nauseous but she forced herself to watch. The man straightened and when he did, he saw Lauren, his expression turning guilty.

Suddenly everything she'd believed about her mother's death changed. He was checking her mother's pulse and there was a gun on the floor. It wasn't in her mother's hand. It was on the carpet right beside the man's knee. He'd clearly put the weapon down a second before.

Her mother had not killed herself.

The man kneeling beside her had killed her.

And that man was Armando.

LAUREN FLEW OFF THE COUCH, the blanket falling to the floor beside her, her hands over her mouth. Armando jumped to his feet.

"It was you!" she cried. "You killed her! You killed my mother. You were there and I saw you."

"No, that's not how it happened." He started toward her. "Please, Lauren, let me explain—"

"No, no, no… There's nothing to explain. Not now." She slapped a hand over her mouth as if she were about to throw up. "Oh, my God," she said from around her fingers. "No wonder you didn't want to help me remember…."

"You don't understand—"

She pushed past him with an anguished cry and flew up the stairs. He ran behind her, then hopped over the railing to cut her off, but he didn't have a chance. The bedroom door slammed a second before he could reach for it and he heard her throw the lock a moment later.

"Open the door, Lauren. Please! We need to talk."

"There's nothing to talk about," she screamed from the other side. "You were there! I remember it all."

He shook the knob furiously. This was just as bad as he'd imagined it would be.

"You don't understand," he said. "You don't know what happened or why I was there. Let me in and I'll explain."

Nothing but silence answered him. Knowing it would do no good but helpless to think of anything else, he pounded on the door and cried her name. The quiet that continued frightened him. "Lauren, open this door or I'm going to knock it down. Do you hear me?"

He rattled the knob again and cursed. Then, before he could think about it anymore, he put his shoulder to the door and pushed.

The house was old and the woodwork was solid. Nothing budged. He thrust against it again, this time harder, but the results were the same. He called out her name once more. "Lauren. I mean it! Open the door!"

A new fear rose as the silence built. He told himself he had no basis for the thought, but logic no longer mattered. All he could imagine was the sight of Lauren lying on the floor, as pale and weak as she'd been after drinking the poisoned tea. She'd thought of herself as the daughter of a suicide victim for years and even though that hadn't been the case, the psychology of the situation had clearly soaked in. Family members of suicide victims were even more likely to kill themselves.

Armando took a step back, then he charged the door and kicked with all his might. The frame splintered. He gave the door a second push and it fell.

A ghostly flutter of movement caught his eye. He jerked his head toward it, his heart leaping into his throat.

The window was open and in the breeze, the curtain waved.

Lauren was nowhere to be seen.

CHAPTER FOURTEEN

LAUREN'S FINGERS BURNED where she'd scraped the skin raw. Jumping from her window to the balcony left of the bedroom hadn't been a major leap but she'd almost missed. Catching herself at the last minute, she swallowed a scream as she heard Armando break down the door. The minute he realized she was gone, he would run to the other room. Her sanctuary would only last a moment longer. She had to decide what to do.

The lights came on in the room behind her and she reacted without thought, just as she had when the bridge had broken. She let go.

The bougainvillea below cushioned her fall, but the drop was still enough to jolt her.

She took a second to gather herself and thrust her feet into the shoes she'd thrown out first, then she took off running, Zue's bag strapped across her shoulders. She had no idea where she was going. All she wanted to do was get away from Armando.

How could she have been so wrong?

Stepping on one of her untied shoelaces, she stumbled, almost going down. She managed to regain her balance but she knew it'd be a long time—if ever—before she got her heart back on a level plane. Stunned by what she'd learned, she couldn't help but think about the moments that had passed just prior. Armand's tender offer to help made his betrayal sting even more sharply. She couldn't believe it. The whole episode was like one of her nightmares, the painful reality too hard to bear.

The sound of footsteps in the darkness behind her took everything but escape from her mind. Gripping her bag, she pushed herself to find an extra measure of speed. It came to her from somewhere and she fled into the night.

ARMANDO SEARCHED THE ALLEYS and nearby streets for more than two hours, but Lauren was nowhere to be found. Picking up the telephone after he returned to the house, he dialed Meredith's number.

"It's me," he said when she answered. "I've got some bad news and some that's even worse."

She listened without comment as he explained what had happened. When he finished, she sighed. "You did the best you could, Armando. If she's gone, she's gone."

He pounded the countertop with his fist. "Dammit, Meredith, I should have helped her at the very beginning. If I had, this wouldn't have happened."

"You're right," Meredith agreed. "She would have taken off even earlier."

"Please!"

"It's the truth, Armando! Once she remembered you were there, what did you expect her to do?"

"But I told her I would help her!" His voice cracked.

"And you still can. We have options,"

she said. "Maybe she'll come back on her own—"

"And maybe she won't! Either way, she isn't safe. Especially if she goes back to Dallas."

"I'll put someone at the airport. We can pick her up before she can even leave the terminal."

"And what if her father gets to her first?"

Meredith didn't answer and, in her silence, Armando sensed trouble. "What is it?" he asked with alarm.

"Well, it might be nothing but I started thinking about Daniel Cunningham...."

"And?"

"I checked with some contacts," she said. "He isn't well regarded within the service, Armando. In fact, there are rumors, he may be on his way out."

"Stanley told Lauren he was up for a promotion."

"He lied," she said. "Or maybe he was lied *to*. Either way, it doesn't matter. Cunningham isn't the all-American patriot he appears to be. There are questions about his service and those questions started in Peru."

"Where is he now?"

"I don't know," she said. "He was stationed in Pakistan, but they called him back last week. He's somewhere between there and Washington."

Armando thought of the blond hiker he'd seen. Could he have been the attaché Armando had known all those years ago? Was that why the man had looked familiar? Armando strained to remember the hiker's face.

Meredith's voice pulled him back from the task. "I don't know what to tell you, Armando. I have a feeling Cunningham's involved, but how or why, I can't say."

"I agree," he said tersely. "But what in the hell am I going to do about it? If I can't find Lauren, none of this will matter. Someone wants her dead and whoever they are and whatever their reasons, they're going to keep trying until they're successful."

AT FIRST, LAUREN THOUGHT the morning's bright sun was what had woken her up, then the long, low whistle of the Aquas train broke the morning silence one more time and she realized her mistake. Scrambling awkwardly to her feet, she grabbed her bag and fought her way from under the debris where she'd spent the last few hours hidden from view.

At some point, she'd figured out the train was her only hope because there was no other way to leave Aquas Caliente. She had to catch the early departure to Cuzco or she was going to be trapped.

The streets were a maze, but she managed to wind her way to the center of the village. As she neared the station, she saw the row of vendors whose presence she'd noted the day before. They'd already begun to set up their stalls. Her gaze darting over the people along the sidewalk, she picked out a young woman selling embroidered hats and bags. A moment later, she was standing in front of the young girl.

The conversation took only a few minutes. Lauren handed over her money and the girl took off, leaving Lauren to watch over her wares. She quickly returned with Lauren's train ticket in her hand. Lauren thanked her, gave her five extra pesos, then bought one of her hats, too. Cramming her hair beneath the scratchy wool, she eased back into the shadows and waited.

THE RELIEF ARMANDO FELT when he finally spotted Lauren was like nothing he'd ever experienced before. A combination of anger, joy and confusion mixed inside of him, and it was all he could do to stop himself from running straight for her. The thought of her hiding all night, scared and worried, had driven him back to the streets the minute after he'd ended the call with Meredith. He'd combed every inch of Aquas, his search concluding at the train station.

His plan had been to take her back to the house, but watching from across the tracks, he hesitated now. Lauren was past the scared-and-worried stage and heading straight for terrified and hysterical. If he tried to grab her here, there was no telling what might happen. Drawing attention was the last thing he wanted to do.

Melding into a crowd of grungy hikers, Armando followed them to the ticket office. With the kids between himself and where Lauren hid, he bought a pass for the next train, then joined another group edging toward the platform.

A piercing whistle announced the train's imminent arrival, the engine deafening as it came into the station proper. Out of the corner of his eye, he watched Lauren emerge from her hiding place. Striding from behind the vendors' stalls, she made her way toward the boarding area on the other side, committing the amateur's mistake by keeping her head down and her eyes to the ground. She didn't know better but she should have been looking for him.

His gaze swinging over the waiting crowd, Armando fell straight into his target mode, his nerves on edge, his body on alert. He was hunting, only this time he wanted to keep his prey safe instead of stalking it.

The locomotive stopped. The first car

momentarily blocked his view but Armando was prepared. He pushed ahead of the hikers and leaped inside it, racing to the windows on the opposite side to keep Lauren in sight.

He spotted her immediately. She was wedged in the middle of the crowd, moving forward as it moved toward the second car. His eyes on the hat she'd bought to hide her hair, he tracked her slow but steady progress. She could disguise the blond hair and blue eyes, but the mixture of strength and vulnerability that ran through her character struck him anew. She'd not only overcome a trauma that few people understood, she'd actually become a stronger, better person because of it.

She was a survivor. A beautiful survivor.

He felt his gaze soften. He loved Lauren and regardless of what happened between them—either now or in the future—that love was not going to change.

The crowd swelled and she was carried into the railcar behind him. Armando started to turn away but something caught his eye. He studied the mass of people, his eyes passing from one face to another.

They pushed forward like a herd of sheep but then, in the center of the flock, one person fought the movement and stood still.

Armando's eyes narrowed as he focused directly on the man.

He wore jeans and a blue T-shirt, the writing on it obscured by the scruffy black backpack that weighed down one broad shoulder. He was blond and he was dirty and when he caught Armando's gaze, he held it with pale blue eyes. He was the German from Machu Picchu and Armando remembered why he had looked familiar. He'd seen him at the café in Rojo, as well.

He wasn't Daniel Cunningham.

His name was Frankle Gunther.

Their paths had crossed once before. He was an assassin, too.

LAUREN SETTLED IN HER SEAT and looked around nervously. No one was paying her any attention and she felt herself relax, but the train had yet to pull out of the station. She wouldn't be convinced she was safe until they were in motion and maybe not even then.

The car filled, and she replayed the arguments she'd made with herself in the hours that had passed since she'd left the house. The conclusions she'd jumped to had begun to feel more and more wrong. Her sense that Armando might have been involved with her mother's death had begun to fade and the impulse that had sent her fleeing didn't feel as right as it had back then. She found herself going over the arguments once again.

If Armando was trying to kill her now, then why had he saved her life twice?

He'd been forced to, she'd told herself, because there had been too many witnesses for him to refuse. Manco had expected him to argue about caring for her after the fall and the people at the clinic would have been shocked if he'd done nothing after she'd drunk the tea. He'd helped her but only because he'd had no other choice.

He'd told her himself that her death *had* to look like an accident.

But why kill her in the first place?

The answer to that question lay in her past. If she'd left it alone, he would never have been forced to go after her, but she'd persisted and so he'd had to get rid of her to protect himself.

He'd been paid to kill her mother.

Someone, probably in the Peruvian government, had wanted her dead and he'd agreed to do the job, never thinking he'd have to deal with a witness. The only reason he'd spared her back then was that she'd been a child. He hadn't been able to shoot a ten-year-old girl and he'd thought she would forget the details. He'd put the gun in Margaret's hand, then had slipped away and left Lauren to be found by her father.

She let her head fall to the headrest, a moan escaping her lips as she looked out the window. The night she and Armando had made love, she'd thought she'd found someone who could accept her for who she really was. Someone who'd love her no matter what. To wake up to this nightmare was doubly cruel.

He'd played with her.

If she hadn't left when she had, he would have murdered her.

He was a killer.

Or was he?

Everything hinged on that one question.

She felt as if she were losing her mind, the tiny shreds of sanity she'd had left disappearing out the window. She'd come to Peru to uncover her past and instead she'd exposed secrets she hadn't even imagined existed.

The train chugged into motion, the noise of the wheels on the tracks competing with the whistle as it sounded once more. Soot, fine and black, drifted in through the open windows.

The scenery blurred as they picked up speed: the red tiled roofs, the thick jungle, the mountaintops. Lauren thought she couldn't see because the train, just like her thoughts, was moving too fast, but then she realized she was crying. Too weary to do anything else, she let the tears fall.

She felt as if she were going crazy but, after a while, she decided she didn't need to act that way, too. She stood up and made her way to the front of the car to the bathroom to wash her face. The door was locked. Swaying with the motion of the train, she prepared herself to wait in the aisle, but without any warning, a crushing anxiety hit her full force. She told herself she was being paranoid, yet there was no mistaking the feeling.

Someone's eyes were on her.

She wanted to run—as fast as she could—but she made herself stay put. There was nowhere for her to go anyway. She was trapped until the train stopped.

She allowed herself one quick look over her shoulder.

A mother and child in the first row. Two farmers in the third. A tourist in the fourth seat and a hiker in the sixth. No one was even looking at her.

Her stomach rolling from the spurt of

adrenaline, she closed her eyes and gripped the bar beside the bathroom door.

When she opened her eyes, a tall blonde stood beside her. He smiled down at her, and she automatically started to smile back. Then she looked at his hand.

He held a gun and it was pointed at her.

"Step outside to the space between the cars," he said in a thick German accent. "I don't want to have to kill anyone else besides you."

CHAPTER FIFTEEN

BEFORE ARMANDO COULD MAKE his move, the man allowed the crowd to swallow him once more and Armando lost sight of him. Gunther was obviously there to kill Lauren and the only thing between him and that goal was Armando. Pushing through the waiting passengers, Armando ignored their startled looks and protestations as he waded through the now full car.

The train took off before he could locate the German. As Armando started out the door at the rear of his car, however, he watched in horror as the killer walked up to Lauren. She seemed oblivious until he spoke to her, but her eyes widened with fright before he pushed her out the door.

Armando didn't wait to see what happened next.

He ran out to the platform between his car and the next. Beneath him, the tracks passed in a haze of speed. The sight barely registered. He jumped without another thought to the danger. Landing, he opened the door and raced through it, but when he reached the platform where he expected to see Lauren and the German, it was empty.

Armando paused, the possible scenarios racing through his head as fast as the train. Had he pushed her off? If he had, where was he now?

Armando had no answers. All he could do was keep going.

When he reached the fourth car, he caught a glimpse of Lauren's hat just before the door at the other end closed. Gunther was taking her through the train, probably to the rear. If he shot her on the last platform and pushed her off, no one would see it.

Armando noted the detail with cold satisfaction.

The thought should have chilled him, but it actually made him feel better. His mind was working like Gunther's and that was how he needed to be thinking if he had half a chance at saving Lauren's life. He pushed through the cars and continued toward the rear of the train.

LAUREN WALKED AS SLOWLY as she could, but no one even looked up as they passed. With the barrel of a pistol stuck into her spine, she wasn't about to cry out, either.

She didn't think pulling attention to herself would have helped anyway. The man's pale eyes and dispassionate demeanor told her this was simply a job to him and nothing more. He'd shoot her—and anyone else who got in his way—then he'd vanish. No one would be the wiser. The suggestion passed through her mind that Armando might have sent him, but she barely gave it notice. Deep down, she knew she was wrong.

Still, the thought unnerved her and she stumbled. The German poked her with the gun, harder than was necessary, and whispered roughly in her ear, his hand painfully tight upon her elbow. "Don't try anything stupid. It won't do you any good."

A few minutes later, they entered the final car. It was empty and she hesitated, but he pushed her forward with a grunt. "Keep going."

Her mouth went dry with fear. There was nowhere else *to* go except the platform at the back. She'd managed not to look down each time they'd switched to a new car but she knew the train was at top speed now.

She realized immediately what that meant. He didn't have to shoot her. If he pushed her off, she'd hit the rocks on either side of the tracks and no one would see it happen. By the time anyone knew she was missing—again—she'd be long dead.

Another suicide for her father to handle.

The idea made her sad and then angry, and suddenly she decided she'd had enough. If this jerk wanted her dead, then by God, he was going to have to work for it.

"Keep going!" Another brutish push of

the gun accompanied his order. "I said don't stop."

She refused to move, the pistol digging into her so hard she expected to see it come out the other side. Slowly she turned around and stared him straight in the eye.

"This is it," she proclaimed. "I'm not going out on that platform. I know what you want to do."

He smiled coldly. "You think I won't shoot you right here?"

"No," she answered. "That's not what I think. I'm sure you'd be happy to shoot me right here, but if that's what you're going to do, then do it and get it over with. I'm not going to let you push me off. No way. I won't let you make this look like a suicide."

He narrowed his eyes. "What makes you think that's what I want?"

"Because it's the truth," a voice said from behind them. "But she's right. It's not going to happen."

Lauren's mouth fell open as she heard Armando speak, fear, relief and confusion all washing over her in a wave.

The man beside her whirled but Lauren didn't wait to see what he would do next. She jumped on his back and wrapped her legs around his waist, her hands twisting in his hair.

The man screamed, lurching to one side in an effort to brush her off against the seats. He didn't have a chance. She hung on with every ounce of strength she had as Armando joined the fight. Grabbing the gun the stranger still gripped, Lauren twisted his fingers backward until she heard several crack. He let out another howl, then the three of them went down with a crash, Lauren on the bottom, Armando on the top.

The air left her lungs in a rush as her head bounced against the filthy floor. Explosions of light burst behind her eyelids.

"Give me the pistol," Armando cried as he landed a punch on the German's square jaw. "Lauren! Pass it to me!"

She opened her eyes in time to see Armando strike the man again, but her attacker was bigger and heavier. It was only a matter of time before he got himself together and began to hit back.

"Lauren, please!"

Their eyes locked over the other man's head and Lauren blinked. Armando was rescuing her, she thought in a daze. He was trying to help.

"Give me the gun, Lauren!" Armando's voice was fading. She could barely hear him as the edges of her vision began to go black. "Give me the gun or shoot the bastard yourself!"

Her mind went fuzzy. She couldn't feel her fingers, then she realized why. Her arm was pinned beneath her.

Armando called her name again but it was cut off before he could finish, the other man landing a hard right to Armando's jaw. His head snapped back, then Lauren felt everything shift and her arm was freed.

She pressed the gun against the blonde and pulled the trigger.

ARMANDO FELT GUNTHER JERK before his scream filled the train, his shriek full of agony as he grabbed his leg. Lauren tossed the gun to Armando, who jumped to his feet.

He held the pistol two inches from the German's head. "Get up, you son of a bitch." When he didn't move, Armando kicked him. In the leg that was bleeding.

He cursed but rose to his knees. Armando prodded him again. "On your feet."

Using the nearest bench, the man pulled himself up, his face a mask of pain and fury. Armando pulled off his belt and threw it to Lauren. "Tie his hands and make it tight enough to turn them purple. When you finish, get away from him."

She did as he instructed.

"Turn around and walk to the back," Armando said to the German. "We're getting off then you're going to answer some questions."

"I won't talk."

Armando smiled. "Would you like to bet on that?"

The killer began to limp toward the back. Armando held his hand out to Lauren. She seemed to waver and his heart buckled, but she finally took his fingers. He wanted to stop and kiss her to take away the shards of doubt that lingered in her eyes, but there was no time. "Did he hurt you?"

"I'm fine."

"Stay behind me," he said out of the corner of his mouth. "You wounded him pretty good but he's strong. Don't take your eyes off him, especially after we get off."

She wore an expression of fear, but she nodded gamely, his opinion of her courage going up another notch. "When does the train stop next?"

"It doesn't," Armando answered. "We're jumping."

Her answer this time didn't sound as enthusiastic, but she didn't let go of his hand.

They followed the German and his trail of blood to the rear of the car.

"Open the door." Armando gestured toward the door's lock with the pistol. "Then step outside."

The man complied and, a few moments after that, the three of them stood on the platform, the wind whipping at their clothes and hair, the trees rushing by. Armando motioned for Lauren to come closer.

"We're coming to a switchback," he yelled above the noise. "The train will slow. When it does, you're going first and taking the gun. I'll push him off then jump behind him. If he even looks like he wants to run, shoot him again."

She nodded grimly and he handed her the pistol. Two seconds later, he jerked his head toward the railing. "Get ready."

The train braked abruptly and the cars bumped with a riotous clang. The sound filled the air as Armando screamed, "Now!"

She didn't hesitate. Springing from the steps where she'd been waiting, she hit the ground, rolled two times then jumped to her feet, the gun in her hand and ready.

Armando turned to the other assassin. A belligerent expression came over his features and he began to shake his head. Armando turned on one foot, then lashed out, catching the man just below the knee on the leg that had been shot. He crumpled into a ball and Armando pushed him off the train. A second later, he followed.

THE MAN WHO'D TRIED to kill her hit the ground hard. He didn't try to get up, much less do any running, but Lauren kept the gun pointed at him. Armando landed only a few feet away. He was standing and by the German's side before she had time to react.

A heavy stillness replaced the train's roar as the last car vanished behind the curve. She came toward them, but gave the blond man a wide berth.

Armando's eyes stayed on the wounded man as he spoke to her. "Keep the gun on us," he instructed. "Don't worry about aiming. Just shoot if he tries anything."

Lauren nodded, then stood by and watched as he ripped open the leg of the jeans the man wore. A painful red streak had been drawn down his thigh from his hip to his knee. The bullet had barely grazed him and the blood loss was minimal.

Armando stood and, to Lauren's amazement, addressed the man by name. "Get up, Gunther. We're going for a walk."

When the killer raised his head, Armando pointed to the tracks.

He stayed where he was. "I'm not going anywhere."

Armando squatted again. The two men were now eye to eye. "You do know who I am, don't you?"

The German stared at him.

"Come on, Gunther. You're hurting my feelings. We met once in South Africa. A long time ago. My name is Armando Torres." He leaned closer. "I used to be known by something else. You might call it my nom de guerre. It's probably what you'd remember me by. I always thought it was silly but someone used it once and it stuck. You know how those things happen."

The pale blue eyes didn't blink.

Armando leaned closer and said something in the man's ear. Lauren only caught two words.

Doctor and *muerte*.

This time there was no mistaking the other man's reaction. He recoiled in fear, his thick lips hanging open.

"Get up," Armando ordered softly. "And start walking."

The German stumbled to his feet with as much quickness as he could muster. Dragging his leg, he climbed up the incline and started down the path between the rails, his hands still bound behind his back. With every other step, he glanced over his shoulder and sent Armando a nervous look.

They followed, Lauren shaking with shock and confusion. "You…you know him?" she finally managed to say.

Armando nodded. "His name is Frankle Gunther. He's a second-rate hired gun."

She stopped abruptly. "What?"

"He's a hit man." Armando tugged her back into motion. "But not a very good one."

"Who would send someone like that after me?"

"I don't know," Armando answered. "But I intend to find out."

She absorbed the information, then spoke again. "I guess I owe you another thank you. I've lost track of how many times you've saved my life."

"You wouldn't have been on that train except for me," he answered. "I forced you to flee. You had no other choice."

This time it was Armando who pulled them to a stop, his hand on her arm as the German continued ahead of them. "I know why you ran, Lauren, but please believe me. I didn't kill your mother. If you accept nothing else as the truth, you must accept that. I swear to you on my grandfather's soul. I was at the party that night, but I did not kill your mother."

"Why were you at the party? What were you doing kneeling beside her then?"

"I promise I'll explain everything to you." He pointed to the man ahead of them. "After I deal with him."

She nodded, knowing she couldn't hold onto the remnants of her previous suspicions—he'd proved her point by rescuing her again. "I understand," she said. "But just tell me this. She didn't kill herself, did she? And there was no burglar...."

"No," he said. "She didn't kill herself. She was murdered, but not by an intruder."

"Did he do it?" Her voice broke as she indicated the German.

"I don't know," Armando said. "But I'll find out. He's going to tell me, whether he wants to or not."

An hour later, they were back on the out-skirts
of Aquas Caliente. Armando took them down the twisted alleyways and back-streets of the village, back to the Busta-mantes' door. Lauren stood by numbly as he unlocked the gate and shoved the barely standing German inside the stuccoed walls of the courtyard. Dragging himself past them, he crumpled into one of the bushes that lined the wall.

Lauren looked down at him dispassion-ately. "Will he be okay?"

"I'll tend to the wound," Armando said. "It's nothing."

Before coming back to Peru, she would have been horrified by the treatment they'd given the man, but now she barely let it cross her mind. Even if he hadn't shot her mother, whatever happened to him was deserved. He would have killed her without Armando's intervention.

"How will you get him to talk?" she asked.

Armando didn't answer. He simply looked at her with eyes that were different from the ones she'd gazed into a few hours before when their heads had been lying on the same pillow. It took her a second to understand the change but when she did, she was finally glad to know the truth.

Armando was a killer *and* a healer.

She'd seen one side and now she was seeing the other.

CHAPTER SIXTEEN

ARMANDO ENTERED THE DEN a few hours later. Lauren stopped beside the window where she'd been waiting and stared at him. He looked exhausted and disgusted, a streak of something on the knees of his pants. A catch formed in her throat.

"Do you want to hear it from him or from me?"

She started to answer him, then she hesitated. She didn't know what she wanted.

He took pity on her. "If you'll believe me," he suggested, "let me tell you. It would be…easier that way."

She came from behind the couch and sat down. "What did he say?"

Armando took the chair on the other side of the coffee table. "Someone paid him to come here and kill you. Someone from the States."

She put her hand to her open mouth then spoke from behind her fingers. "Who would do such a thing? And why?"

"I can only guess," he answered. "At both of those questions. He didn't have the answers or I would know by now."

His answer signified a confidence in his interrogation skills that she wouldn't let herself consider. "How will we ever find out?"

"It won't be easy. The money was washed."

She frowned and he explained.

"Electronic transfers were made from the U.S. to France and then to Germany. The cash went through so many hands there's no way to tell where it originated."

She thought about what that meant, then her focus turned. "And my mother?"

"He knew nothing about that."

"Are you sure—"

Armando cut her off. "He wasn't lying,

Lauren. Believe me, I got the truth from him."

She shivered lightly. "Did he give you any details? Did he cut the bridge? What about the tea—"

He didn't let her finish her questions. "Gunther paid Joaquin to approach you at the train station and take you to the bridge. The rope had already been weakened. All Peña had to do was cut one strand to make it break when your weight reached the middle. When you survived the fall, Gunther had to go for plan B. Which was to bribe Manco to kill you."

"But he saved me—"

Armando smiled grimly. "Manco thought you'd be more valuable to him alive. He planned on ransoming you, instead. He knew sooner or later someone would start looking for you and he thought he could use you himself. When Gunther discovered Manco's twist, he wasn't pleased, especially when he learned you were with me."

"Why did Manco let you take me?"

"He didn't have a choice," Armando said

flatly. "Once I showed up and knew about you, his ransom scheme was spoiled. The two men who came from the village and told me about you saved your life. In the meantime, he kept giving you *la planta durmiente* to keep you sedated, which would explain your adverse reaction to it when you got more of it later on in the tea. When the extract finally wore off and left your body, so did your amnesia."

"What about the tea?"

"That was Gunther, too. He'd already killed Joaquin to keep him quiet so he had to find someone else to help. Joaquin's brother suggested Beli and supplied the poison. Gunther traded the kid some drugs to get him to put the *durmiente* extract into your mug and leave the pill bottle beside you to make it look like a suicide attempt. It was easy for him. Zue has keys to the cabinet, too, so I'm sure Beli sneaked hers one day and got the pill case. Lucky for you he stole the pills and only put the *durmiente* in your tea. If he'd combined the two, we wouldn't be having this conversation." He grimaced. "I didn't believe him when he said he went with Zue to visit her sister but I didn't press him hard enough. He must have stayed at the clinic."

"Do you think Zue knows?"

"She covered for him, so who can say? I'd like to think she believes he's innocent, but family comes first down here." He paused. "Gunther was going to try something at Picchu but the opportunity never came up. There were more people there than he'd anticipated. He followed us home, though. He was watching the house. When you ran off, he waited. He knew you'd try and take the train."

Lauren held herself tensely, anxiety keeping her frozen in place. "Who did this, Armando? Who hates me so much they want me dead?"

"It hasn't got anything to do with hate, Lauren."

"Then what?"

"I told you earlier. This is about your mother." He came to where she sat and took her hands. They were freezing. "This is about your mother…and your father."

His answer turned her inside out. In the middle of the night, when she couldn't sleep, she'd wondered about this herself, but the idea had seemed so horrific she'd always pushed it aside. "You think my father is behind this?"

"He's the one who made you think your mother killed herself, Lauren. Why else would he do something like that?"

"But he said—"

"You heard them arguing," he said softly, his voice filled with pity. "They were talking about money. She'd put his ability to make a living on hold. She told him she loved her country. He resented having to give up so much."

In spite of her doubts, Lauren started shaking her head. "You don't know my father. He couldn't have killed her, especially over something as petty as money."

Armando continued as if she hadn't spoken. "They argued, he shot your mother, then he must have heard me coming. He hid until I left. Then he came back in, wiped down the weapon and wrapped her fingers around it. After that, he turned to comfort you."

She stared at him and let the story roll over her.

"I was there, Lauren. I came into that room but your mother was already dead. There was a gun *on the floor beside her.* You started screaming and I left, then your father came *back* in. He made up the story of her suicide and planted it in your memory." Armando blinked, looked away, then faced her again. "That's why he didn't want you to come down here—he couldn't have the two of us compare stories. Why else would he have kept track of me? Why keep you away from me? Somehow he knew I was there that night. Having the State Department issue the false press release just reinforced everything. He made you feel ashamed of what supposedly took place so you'd keep it a secret."

She fell silent, her pulse beating painfully, her head spinning with confusion.

"But you questioned your memories yourself," he pointed out. "You *knew* something was wrong with your recollections. Some were specific, some were vague. You remembered some things and couldn't figure out others…. That's because your memories of her suicide are false. You understood that even though you didn't know why."

"How could he be so certain I wouldn't remember what really happened?"

"He told you that night she killed herself, he made sure you saw the gun in her hand, and that's all you heard, over and over. He's a well-known psychiatrist, but even more importantly, he was your father. There is no greater authority figure in a child's life than his parent. If Daddy says it's so, then it's so. You bought the story because of who he is. He had to cover up his part in her death."

"But why?" she asked in an anguished voice. "Why would he do something like that? My father loved my mother. He wasn't happy, but he would never have killed her." She didn't want to think about whatever Armando was still hiding but she couldn't ignore it any longer. "You were there, too," she said, her voice filling with a suspicion she didn't conceal. "How do I know *you're* telling me the truth?"

He stared at her.

"You're going to have to tell me sooner or later," she warned. "Your past is part of who you are. If I don't know it, I don't know you. And if I don't know you, then I can never trust you."

"I guess we're going to have to stop right here, then," he said reluctantly, "because I cannot explain."

"I would never tell—"

He put a finger across her lips. "There's a man in the garage behind us who can keep secrets much better than you, Lauren. He was taught to because his life depends on it. But he answered every one of my questions because he didn't have a choice. If someone wanted to find out the truth from you, you would do the same, only much quicker. Too many could suffer if my activities were revealed."

She didn't want to understand. But she did.

"But you must know something more to believe my father killed her," she insisted. "What would have been his motive?"

He studied the floor for a moment, then raised his eyes, a resigned reluctance filling their depths. "There was a double agent inside the Embassy, Lauren. Someone was stealing American secrets from confidential files and selling them to the Peruvians. If not your mother, then it had to be either your father or Daniel Cunningham. I was sent to figure out the mole's identity, then take care of the situation."

"Who sent you?"

"I can't tell you that."

"How were you going to 'take care' of it?"

"I can't tell you that, either," he answered. "The important question is why."

"All right," she said. "Then tell me why."

"Moles are dangerous. They destroy one important reason for having a consulate, which is to engender better relationships between countries. Things break down when a mole is in place."

Lauren stared at Armando, her mouth slowly falling open, the importance of what he'd just said ringing inside her head like a bell that wouldn't stop. "Did you say mole?"

He spoke patiently. "It's a term we use to describe someone who's selling information. No one knows who they are—"

"I know what a mole is," she said in wonder. "But I didn't understand…."

He frowned. "What are you talking about, Lauren?"

"There was a crow in my dream," she said excitedly. "Remember? I told you about it and I said it turned into another animal. It was a *mole*."

"And…?"

"I was just a kid. I had to have heard the word—*mole*—otherwise I wouldn't have made the association." She understood suddenly what he'd meant when he'd told her she was the only one who could interpret her dreams.

He nodded with approval. "Whoever

killed your mother had to have been the mole if that's what they were arguing over. They knew she'd reveal their identity."

Armando stood and pulled Lauren to her feet, his arms going around her tightly. He caressed her cheek, then he dropped his hand and captured her fingers again.

"I cannot tell you any more about what I do," he said. "But I *can* give you my heart. And what I think is the truth. You can have them both or reject them both but you can't take one without the other."

Her eyes filled and the words came to her lips unbidden. "I love you."

"I love you, too, *querida*. Ever since I saw you that night, when you were so frightened yet so beautiful… I knew then we'd be connected forever, but I didn't understand how or why."

"I felt the same way, Armando. Even more so, now."

"I agree, but will the truth keep us apart?"

"I don't want it to."

"Then we have to know who really killed *tu madre*." He held her hand tightly.

"We have to go to your father, Lauren. It's the only way we can find out what really happened that night."

ARMANDO MADE TWO PHONE CALLS and, an hour later, they were heading for the train station again. Walking toward the center of town, they were passed by a police car, its sirens cutting through the quiet, its lights flashing as it headed in the opposite direction.

Armando looked down and caught Lauren's eye. "Someone must have had a break-in," he said blandly. "They'll probably find a burglar."

She turned and looked over her shoulder, then she faced him again, her eyes going wide as she understood. He'd phoned the police himself. They would find Gunther and deal with what was left of him.

Two hours later, they were on the train, a different one, of course, but heading down the very same tracks. With lavender circles under her eyes and her shoulders drooping with exhaustion, Lauren rested her head against Armando's shoulder and went to sleep immediately. Armando wasn't as lucky. His thoughts went in circles and refused to let him rest. All he could do was think about the situation that waited for them.

Lauren didn't want to believe her father had had anything to do with her mother's death but, sooner or later, she was going to have to face the truth. Was she tough enough to handle it?

Twenty-four hours before this point, Armando would have said no, but now he wasn't so sure. Lauren had proven herself stronger—mentally and physically—than he'd thought possible. The understanding he'd seen dawn in her eyes when she'd told him her dream proved that all the more.

He loved her, just as he'd confessed.

But they could never have a life together.

She didn't fit into his world and he didn't *want* to fit into hers. His past would always loom between them, as well. It was a weight around his neck that he would carry forever. Anywhere, anytime, he could be recognized. If the wrong person figured out who he was, then his life was worthless. He loved Lauren too much to expose her to that kind of risk.

He put his hand on the crown of her head and pulled her closer, his heart swelling. One way or another, their days together were limited.

THE TRIP PASSED IN A BLUR for Lauren. Once in Cuzco and on the plane, she shut down her mind and simply tried not to think. Fifteen hours later, they were in Dallas. Standing outside the terminal at DFW, waiting for Armando to get them a cab, she blinked and seemed to wake up.

In thirty minutes, she was going to see her father and confront him about the troubled past they shared. She wasn't completely sure she was up to the task, but she had to know what had really happened the night her mother had died. She'd come too far to stop now.

A cold wind picked at her hair, lifting

strands to toss them into her eyes. Holding them back, she pulled her jacket closer and climbed into the yellow cab, whose door Armando now opened. He followed her in and they pulled out into traffic.

"Gotta address?" The cabbie looked at her in his rearview mirror.

She could feel Armando's stare as she answered in a wooden voice. "Nine-oh-six Lawndale Drive."

He took her hand in his. "Are you all right?"

"I don't know," she answered painfully. "This all seems like one of my dreams…a nightmare. I want to know what actually happened but, at the same time, I'm afraid to find it out."

"You wouldn't be human if you didn't have mixed feelings," he said. "This isn't an easy situation, either way." He squeezed her fingers. "I'll be with you, though. Whatever he has to say, we're going to hear it together and that's a promise you can count on."

They pulled into a suburban office

complex some twenty minutes later, the tree-lined parking lot quiet and unassuming, the difference between where they were and where they'd been astonishing. Lauren got out of the cab, but her feet refused to take her farther. After all this time, was she about to find out the truth?

Armando put his hand on her back and his touch gave her the strength she needed. They started down the sidewalk and went inside a moment later.

Her father's suite was on the ground floor, the waiting room peaceful and elegant with a couch and two chairs in muted colors. In the corner sat a small waterfall that filled the silence with the soothing sounds of trickling water. Walking toward a series of buttons on the wall beside another door, Lauren punched the one that had her father's name beside it then turned to Armando. "It may be a while if he's in session."

"That's fine," he said. Lauren had wanted to call and tell her father they were on the way but Armando had stopped her.

She'd understood his reasons and complied, reluctantly.

They were both surprised when the door opened a second later. Lauren immediately jumped up from the chair she'd just taken and rushed forward. Armando followed, but Lauren was conscious of nothing except how her father looked.

Something was dreadfully wrong.

As tight as a loaded spring, he seemed ready to strike, his eyes full of distrust, his voice stilted. The knot in his tie had been jerked to one side and his shirt pocket actually had a rip in it. When he made no move to come forward, she dropped her arms and hesitated. "Daddy?"

"Lauren!" He said her name with what sounded like anguish.

Her mouth dry, all she could do was smile. "We...we weren't sure exactly when we were going to arrive so I didn't call. I hope that's okay. We thought we might surprise you."

"You certainly did that."

A small silence filled the moment, then

Armando moved in closer. He put his left hand on Lauren's shoulder and held out his other one and introduced himself. "Dr. Stanley, I am Armando Torres. It is a pleasure to make your acquaintance."

Her father came a step closer and took Armando's hand. "I appreciate all you did for my daughter, Doctor."

"I was glad to be of service."

The movement put her father at Lauren's side and, all at once, his arms were around her in a hug so tight she couldn't move. "I'm so glad you came home! I've been so worried about you—"

She started to answer him but he tightened his embrace even more. "Run!" he whispered urgently, his voice hoarse. "Run right now. Daniel Cunningham is behind the door. He's going to kill us—"

Before he could finish, chaos broke out. Ripped from her embrace, he cried out and stumbled backward, his arms flailing, his feet going out from beneath him. Lauren reached for him, but Armando reacted faster, grabbing her and pushing her behind himself.

"Don't bother to protect her now. It won't do you any good."

A tall blond man stood behind her father, one broad hand holding him still, a large black pistol in the other. His blue eyes were cold. If her father hadn't warned her, Lauren wasn't sure she would have recognized Daniel Cunningham.

Overweight and overindulged, the middle-aged man looked nothing like the handsome attaché she'd had a crush on all those years before. There were bags under his eyes and an empty look inside them that completely chilled her. He turned her father around and began to tape his wrists, throwing Lauren a glare as he did so.

"You've caused me more trouble than you're worth. I thought I took care of the Stanleys and all their problems back in Peru, but here we are again."

He checked his handiwork, then yanked on it and pushed her father to the floor. He fell hard and grunted in pain. With a cry of her own, Lauren started forward but Armando held her back.

"What do you want?" Armando demanded. "Why are you here?"

Daniel Cunningham's gaze held no emotion. "Don't ask questions when you already know the answer, Doctor. You know exactly what I want and exactly why I'm here. I have some loose ends that need to be tied."

"The Stanleys aren't loose ends," Armando replied. "Walk away and you'll be a free man."

"Walking away is not an option. Lauren's trip to understand her past came at a very inconvenient time for me. I'm having a few problems climbing up the State Department's ladder and I'm afraid I can't have that." He shook his head at Armando. "Now you're involved. A few years have passed since we met in Peru. I'm not quite as anxious for friends as I was back then. Now I know who you are and what you do. I don't intend on spending the rest of my life looking over my shoulder."

"You'll never see me again," Armando promised.

"I'm sure you're right." Daniel laughed. "I'd just wake up dead one morning, right?"

"You don't deserve anything else," Freeman said, his voice harsh.

Daniel swung the pistol to Lauren's father and pulled back the hammer. Lauren gasped, the click hideously loud.

"Shut up, Freeman. I'm not ready to deal with you yet and timing is everything." His voice dropped, his anger apparent. "You should have asked Margaret about that."

The change in the way he spoke took Lauren back to that awful night. She'd heard that same arrogant tone when she'd been hiding in her mother's closet. She closed her eyes and drew in an audible breath. When she opened them, she spoke quietly.

"It was you I heard arguing with her, wasn't it?" she said tightly. "You were the mole and she'd found out. You had to shoot her before she could tell."

"I'm afraid you're right," he said. "You always were a sharp little thing."

"You son of a bitch!" Freeman tried to get up. "That's not what you told me! You said—"

Daniel kicked her father, pushing him back down to the floor with a laugh. "What did you expect, Freeman? The truth? C'mon…"

Lauren's shocked eyes jumped to her father's face. "You knew?"

Her father glared at Daniel but he answered her. "He told me right before the party that an assassin was coming after Margaret, but he made me promise not to tell. He said she hadn't wanted me to know so I couldn't let on that I did. She wanted everyone to act normal because they were going to try and catch the man who'd been sent to kill her." His voice broke. "It sounded just like something she'd do so I believed him…."

"Oh, my God. You moved the gun, you told me the lie…." Lauren shot a disbelieving gaze at Armando. They had both been right—and wrong. She turned back to her father in horror. "You set everything up? Why?" Her voice was filled with agony. "Why?"

"It was the only way I could protect you," he cried. "When I found you in the closet, I thought you'd seen everything. I knew if you could identify the killer, he'd come after you next. I wanted to keep you safe. I never suspected Daniel. I panicked...."

Lauren felt the air leave her lungs. She tried to get a breath but couldn't.

"I was only trying to shield you! I didn't know what to do." Her father's eyes pleaded with her for understanding. "I put the gun in her hand, I lied about everything and then I agreed to the fake press release Daniel wrote and gave to the higher-ups at the State Department. All I wanted to do was get us out of the country and away from whoever killed her."

"And who did you think actually did that?" Armando's voice was low.

He turned and met Armando's accusing

stare. "I thought it was you," he said brokenly. "Daniel told me you were an assassin and I believed him."

CHAPTER SEVENTEEN

ARMANDO PULLED LAUREN behind him once again. In the process, he managed to get another two feet closer to Daniel Cunningham. "None of this matters now," he said. "Drop the gun, Cunningham, and step away from it."

Daniel Cunningham ignored Armando's warning. "Gunther must not be the man he used to be. Back in the old days, he was faster and meaner. Are you still in the business, Torres? I'd heard you'd retired, but maybe I should think about hiring you next time I need someone killed."

"There's not going to be a next time," Armando said.

"You're right." Cunningham waved the gun to-ward Lauren and her father. "Because my problems are about to be behind me. There's going to be some other unfortunate deaths in this family—a murder-suicide. The note will explain everything. While we were waiting for you, Dr. Stanley wrote it out. He *did* kill his wife all those years ago and the guilt finally overcame him. He told his troubled daughter, shot her and then turned the gun on himself.

"But you're still going to have one *big* problem."

"And that would be?"

Armando tapped his chest once and moved another inch closer. "Me."

"Not for long."

"You have a lot of confidence in yourself."

"No. I have a gun. I don't need anything else."

This time it was Armando's turn to smile. "I don't even need that."

His right foot shot out, his boot catching Daniel Cunningham's slack jaw right where it met his ear. Lauren screamed but Cunningham didn't make a sound. He simply crumpled to the floor, the pistol dropping from his fingers to bounce once on the carpeted floor. Armando was on top of him before anyone else could move.

He yanked Cunningham's hands behind him. "Get me the tape," he ordered over his shoulder.

Lauren scrambled after the roll and handed it to Armando. Then she turned to her father. With a cry, she ripped the binding from his wrists and then his ankles, their arms going around each other as they both began to talk.

Armando broke up their reunion a second later. "Are your phones working?"

"They are." Lauren's father rubbed his wrists. "You watch him. I'll call the police—"

"No. No police. We need a different set of people here."

Lauren touched her father's arm. "Let Armando handle it, Daddy." Her eyes met Armando's in the space that was between them. "Trust me on this one. He knows what to do."

THEY CAME WITHIN THE HOUR. Lauren had no idea who they were, but Armando gave the people their instructions and, in short order, they cleaned everything up and hauled Cunningham away. They even brought medics to check on her father. As the process played out, she stared at Armando in amazement but he pretended he didn't see her. Who were these people? she wondered but didn't ask. How did he know them? What else did they do?

She turned to her father instead. "How did he find you?" she asked in a broken voice. "How did Daniel know what had happened?"

Sitting in the chair his patients usually took, her father seemed to gather himself.

"I left my phone number with his office when I was checking on you. I guess he got the address from it."

"And Gunther?"

"Is that the man he sent after you?"

She nodded.

"Daniel said he bribed his way out of jail before you two even left the country.

He was proud of the fact that he'd hired someone so good," he said bitterly.

"Well, he wasn't *that* good," Armando broke in. "We're all alive and he'll be picked up as soon as he shows his face at any airport in the world."

Lauren's father stood and extended his hand to Armando. "I owe you more than I can ever repay. You saved my life but more importantly, you protected Lauren, too. What can I do to repay you?"

Armando shook his head. "You owe me nothing," he said. "What's done has been done. If you want to give something to someone, then give Lauren the truth. It's what she deserves."

Before she could say anything, her father turned to her, his eyes filling as he spoke in a broken voice. "He's right. I should have told you what really happened years ago," he said shakily. "Even at the time, I knew I was doing something terrible by lying to you about your mother's death, but I was scared. I wanted to protect you. I hadn't defended her and you were all I had left. Can you ever forgive me?"

"There's nothing to forgive, Dad. Not now. I understand." Lauren squeezed his fingers in reassurance, then she sent Armando a look. "If I had a daughter, I would have felt the same way."

"I didn't do the right thing," he said.

"You did what you thought was best." She leaned over and kissed him. "That's all that matters now."

THEY LEFT THE OFFICE and drove straight to the home Lauren and her father had lived in after coming back from Peru. As he walked inside the elegant foyer, Armando gazed at the gleaming wood floor and expensive rugs. The house fit Lauren perfectly, the fine furnishings and graceful draperies a direct reflection of who she was and how she'd been raised.

It was a far cry from his bungalow in the jungle.

They made their way to the kitchen, where Lauren heated some soup for her father and made sandwiches for them. The psychiatrist seemed overwhelmed by all that had happened and, as soon as he finished eating, he begged their understanding and disappeared down one of the hallways. Lauren sent Armando a look of helpless love, before following her father. She came back a half hour later. She'd been crying, but she finally seemed at peace.

"I had to convince him we'd still be there when he woke up," she said, wiping the corner of her eye with a finger. "He was still apologizing. I forgave him immediately but I don't know if he'll ever forgive himself."

Armando spoke softly. "Guilt is a terrible companion. I hope he won't blame himself for too long. He made a mistake, yes, but he was trying to protect you. It's understandable."

"I agree," she said.

A small silence built between them, then Armando broke it. "We have to talk."

"Can it wait until the morning?"

"I think not," he answered. "I may not be here then."

Lauren frowned, her eyes going a shade darker than he'd ever seen them before. After a second, she said, "Let's go out to the veranda, then. In the garden. It'll be quiet and we won't be disturbed."

With his hand in the small of her back, Armando followed her through the house. They exited through a pair of French doors to a covered patio. Two steps beyond, a lap pool gleamed in the darkness.

Once they were outside, Armando found himself at a loss. He wanted to tell Lauren how much he loved her and how he wanted to be with her for the rest of his life. But he couldn't.

Their relationship was over.

Lauren stepped into his arms and he felt his resolution melt.

"Thank you just doesn't seem like the right thing to say for all you've done for me," she said, her eyes meeting his. "I'm going to need a lifetime to pay you back."

"You don't have to thank me," he said.

"Or pay me back. Anyone else would have done the same."

"That's not true. Your stakes are a lot higher and we both know it. You could have let Daniel do what he wanted to and walked away. It would have made your life a lot simpler."

"That's not who I am."

"You're right," she said. "But I think 'who you are' is a little more complicated than it is for most people."

Armando stiffened but Lauren squeezed his arms and refused to step back. "You can't push me away any longer, Armando. I know the truth now."

"You may think you know, but you don't," he said. "No one can. No one *should*."

"Everything you've ever done, you've done because you wanted to make the world a better place. You told me that yourself. I haven't forgotten what you said that night so don't try and act like you didn't say that."

"I don't want to," he said. "But just as my past can't be changed, neither can my future."

"Don't you mean *our* future?"

He put his hands on her waist. Holding her tight, he looked into her eyes. "We can't be together, Lauren. It won't work."

"You're making excuses."

"I'm telling you the truth. I can't look away when wrongs are done. I can't ignore injustice and oppression."

"I'm not asking you to." She closed her eyes for a moment, then opened them and stared at him. "When I saw you lash out at Daniel, my heart nearly jumped out of my chest. I was terrified he was going to shoot you and in that millisecond before I understood it'd be okay, I wanted to throw myself between you and him. I can't stand the idea of losing you, Armando. But I would never ask you to change."

He kissed her fingers one by one but before he could speak, she stopped him. "Were you lying when you said you loved me?"

"No." He didn't bother to hide his torment.

"If you were, then I'd let you go, but if you really do love me, there's nothing you can say or do that's going to make me let you walk away."

He gave it one last try. "I don't want to live in this world." He tilted his head toward the house behind them. "It's not who I am anymore."

"It isn't who I am, either," she said. "I love the clinic. I want to go back to Peru." She put her arms around his neck and waited a beat. "Is that all you've got? Are there any more excuses?"

He didn't smile. "I can't risk exposing you to my life, Lauren. It's too dangerous. It doesn't matter how much I love you or you love me. I'm a marked man. Some day when I least expect it, someone will find me and I will be gone, just like that."

"You just don't get it, do you?" She brushed her lips over his with a loving touch, then pulled back and looked at him. "You saved my life—in more ways than I can even count. If you hadn't helped me, I'd be stuck where I was and that wasn't a life—it was just an existence full of fears and phobias and God knows what else." She pressed herself against him and kissed him again. "I'm alive when I'm with you, Armando. Alive in a way that I never knew about before I met you. I'd rather have a short time with you than an eternity with anyone else."

He put his hand against her cheek. "Are you sure?" he asked. "Absolutely sure? Once you make the decision, there is no going back."

"I wouldn't want to go back."

"There may be times when I have to leave. You can ask no questions."

"I've lived with questions all my life. I can do it again."

"There may be a day when I leave and don't come back."

"Then we'll have to make the moments we have really count."

"Can you do that?"

"I can't do anything else."

"Are you positive?"

"I've never been more sure of anything in my life," she said. "I love you, Armando.

And I have since the first time I saw you. We were meant to be together forever."

He slipped his hand behind her neck and pulled her to him, her skin warm beneath his touch. "Then I love you, too, *querida*. But as far as I'm concerned, even an eternity isn't long enough. I want you for forever…forever and a day."

HARLEQUIN *Super*ROMANCE®

...there's more to the story!

Superromance.
A *big* satisfying read about unforgettable
characters. Each month we offer *six* very different
stories that range from family drama to adventure
and mystery, from highly emotional stories to
romantic comedies—and much more! Stories
about people you'll believe in and care about.
Stories too compelling to put down....

Our authors are among today's *best* romance
writers. You'll find familiar names and talented
newcomers. Many of them are award winners—
and you'll see why!

If you want the biggest and best
in romance fiction, you'll get it
from Superromance!

Emotional, Exciting, Unexpected...

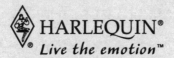

HARLEQUIN®
Live the emotion™

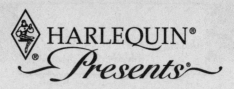

HARLEQUIN® *Presents*

**The world's bestselling romance series...
The series that brings you your favorite authors,
month after month:**

Helen Bianchin...Emma Darcy
Lynne Graham...Penny Jordan
Miranda Lee...Sandra Marton
Anne Mather...Carole Mortimer
Susan Napier...Michelle Reid

and many more uniquely talented authors!

Wealthy, powerful, gorgeous men...
Women who have feelings just like your own...
The stories you love, set in exotic, glamorous locations...

HARLEQUIN® *Presents*

Seduction and Passion Guaranteed!

HPDIR104

Harlequin Historicals®
Historical Romantic Adventure!

From rugged lawmen and valiant knights to defiant heiresses and spirited frontierswomen, Harlequin Historicals will capture your imagination with their dramatic scope, passion and adventure.

Harlequin Historicals . . . they're too good to miss!

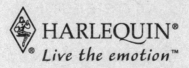

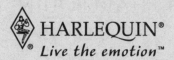